Erma

Book 3 of the Women of the Fellowship Series

Julia A. Royston

Edited by: Claude R. Royston

BK Royston Publishing, LLC

Jeffersonville, IN

BK Royston Publishing
P. O. Box 4321
Jeffersonville, IN 47131
502-802-5385
http://www.bkroystonpublishing.com
bkroystonpublishing@gmail.com

Cover Photo: Joe Goodwin Photography
Cover Design: Bill Lacy

ISBN-13: 978-0692402542
ISBN-10: 0692402543

Printed in the United States of America

Women of the Fellowship Series

 http://bit.ly/jillianbyjuliaroyston

 http://bit.ly/vernicebyroyston

 http://bit.ly/ermabyjuliaroyston

Dedication

This book is dedicated to anyone who thinks that they are now too old for love. You are never too old to give, receive or be loved.

This book is dedicated to my friend and Texas mother, Evangelist Ida B. Johnson Walls. God bless you.

Acknowledgements

First, I acknowledge my Lord and Savior Jesus Christ for giving me all of my gifts and especially my gift to write His words.

My husband who is always supportive, loving and encouraging me to utilize all of my gifts and talents. Thank you honey.

To my mother, Dr. Daisy Foree, who is my best friend, number one cheerleader and always tells me, "hang in there, you can do it." To my father, Dr. Jack Foree, who is never far away from me in spirit and in my heart. I only have to look in the mirror each day to see him.

To Rev. Claude and Mrs. Lillie Royston who support me in everything I do. Especially, Rev. Royston for his careful eye to detail and his sensitive heart to content. This time they are models for real on the cover of this book.

To the rest of my family, I love you and thank you for your prayers, support and love.

Table of Contents

Introduction

In Book 1 of the Women of the Fellowship Series we were introduced to Jillian Forrester, Vernice Washington and Erma Jamison. These three women are different in their looks, occupation and residences but simultaneously, they are alike in that they all three want to be loved.

Jillian is a single professional woman living in Cincinnati, OH who has it all. Her own house, car, corporation, education and money but where is the love?

In Book 2, Vernice is a single mother of a high school senior about to go to college on a full athletic scholarship. Vernice and her son live in windy Chicago going about their daily lives. Vernice works hard at her job striving to get ahead and be promoted. David, Jr. works hard at school wanting to make his mother proud and himself independent.

They attend church and very active in the national organization, The Christian Church World Fellowship Conference. Vernice works on the national planning staff and would love to meet a very nice, Christian man and eventually remarry.

Vernice didn't really want a stepfather for her son because his biological father wasn't a good father.

Now that her son is almost fully grown, she doesn't have to worry about a stepfather for her son, but her desire is only for passionate love in her life.

In Book 3, Ms. Erma Jamison is so happy for her goddaughters because they have found the love and happiness for their lives. While still at the wedding reception of her goddaughter, Jillian Forrester Randolph, a man from her past approaches her to ask if she is now ready for the change in her life with rekindled love.

The Women of the Fellowship Series is all about love for everybody at any age and at any stage.

Julia Royston

Erma

Chapter 1

Erma Jamison loved weddings. She was honored and privileged to be at one of her god-daughter's weddings, Jillian Forrester. Jillian was marrying Byron Randolph. Bishop and Mrs. Randolph along with their twin sons, Byron and Myron Randolph from Indiana had been Erma's longtime church conference friends. Today was not a church conference but a glorious day for a wedding. It had rained earlier so the ground was glistening and the sun was shining. The banquet hall for the reception was decorated beautifully and she was seated at the VIP table along with her longtime friend Frances Thompson. Erma and Frances were to be joined at their table by the groom's parents, Bishop and Mrs. Randolph and the bride's mother, Delores Forrester, a fellow Texan. Ruby Williams and Ida Mae Washington were in attendance but thankfully, not seated at the table with Erma. They had all known each other since childhood but over the years, Erma was no longer friends with Ruby or Ida Mae.

The room was crowded with family, friends, corporate leaders and other well-wishers awaiting the wedding party to enter the beautiful Martin Mahogany Mansion located in downtown Cincinnati. The mansion overlooked the mighty Ohio River. There was a porch that surrounded the building, a grand hall with an entrance that lead to two winding staircases. At the bottom of the staircases, were round tables complete with gold accessories, white covered chairs with gold bows, fine gold china settings along with delicate center pieces at each table. The dark mahogany wood floors and elegant hanging chandeliers complimented the decorations perfectly. There was a full band, dance floor, a table for the honored guests and a never ending buffet of food, drinks and assorted desserts. The feast was fit for a king and queen. The music serenaded everyone as they greeted each other until the wedding party arrived.

"Erma, I thought the church was decorated nice but girl, this room takes my breath away," Frances said leaning over to Erma.

"Yes, honey it is simply lovely," Erma replied.

Bishop and Mrs. Randolph walked over to Erma before taking their seat and Bishop Randolph said, "Erma thank you so much for coming back to Cincinnati from Texas for the wedding, especially since you were just here in April. We greatly appreciate it. You have always supported our sons and we thank you."

"Yes, Erma thanks so much," Mrs. Laura Randolph added.

"Bishop, I wouldn't have missed it for the world. I chased those boys down enough hallways along with Jillian and Vernice. I am glad that I am still alive to help them celebrate accomplishments as grown, successful men," Erma said.

"Me too Erma," Mrs. Laura Randolph added.

"Laura, you look gorgeous in that dress," Erma remarked.

"Thank you. Myron and Vernice haven't set a date yet, but I guess I'll have to get another one real soon for their wedding," Laura replied.

"Yes and I will have to budget for another plane ticket to get back here for that wedding too. They just have to let me know a date and city," Erma said.

"They'll let you know. Myron didn't want to take anything away from Byron's wedding. So Vernice and Myron said they would let everybody know after this wedding," Bishop Randolph stated.

"Yes, they haven't even let me know and I'm in the same city with Vernice," Frances, Vernice's mother stated and continued, "I am so proud of them both and excited for my daughter, grandson and soon to be son in law. Lord help me."

"Lord, help us both," Laura Randolph said as she laughed. The Randolphs left the table and started greeting guests at each table along with Delores, Jillian's mother and Frances, Vernice's mother. Erma remained in her seat and just watched the whole scene. She saw so many faces of people that she recognized and hoped to speak to before the night ended. Erma was seemingly glued to her seat and remembered her own wedding nearly fifty years prior. The scene was nothing this opulent or grand, but the love was there just the same.

Julia Royston

Chapter 2

48 Years prior

"I now pronounce you husband and wife. Harold Jamison you may now kiss your bride," Rev. Russell Smith said to his new son in law.

"Thank you sir, it is my pleasure," Harold Jamison said as he lifted the veil and kissed her until he felt a tap on his shoulder.

It was her father, "You can kiss her some more tonight on the honeymoon. We are hungry and it's time to eat."

The small white church just over the railroad tracks was ablaze with laughter in addition to the heat and could be heard by any passerby in the East Texas town of St. Charles, Texas.

"I am pleased to introduce to you, Mr. and Mrs. Harold Jamison," Rev. Smith said. Erma would have loved to have heard her father say, 'my daughter and son in law at the end' but it didn't happen. Her father probably didn't think it was necessary or want to make the ceremony different from any other girl that he had married in this church. But, Erma was different. Erma was his daughter and only child. Erma wanted to feel special. Erma often wondered what it would be like if she had been born a boy. Would her parents then think she was special?

Erma stood on that small raised stage in that long white lace dress with a small veil now removed and her arm wrapped around the one person who thought she was special enough to marry, Harold Jamison. Harold was a little shy but he was smiling as he looked at Erma who was looking back at him.

Erma and Harold were born in St. Charles, Texas located 15 miles outside of Kilgore and 30 miles from Longview Texas. The trees are tall, the grass is green and the cotton grows wild along the road. It was August of 1970 and one of the hottest summers ever, but that didn't stop them from getting married. Harold had waited two years after they graduated high school to marry her. She was encouraged by her teachers to go to college and in spite of her parent's objections, fulfilled that dream of a two year associates degree in administrative studies.

The groomsmen were Harold's friends from work and the bridesmaids were Erma's best friends for life, Delores, Frances and Ruby minus Ida Mae. Because of the heat, the girls were standing there in light pink dresses and fanning themselves with the small bouquets of flowers that were handpicked from the Smith's flower garden grown for this day.

The ladies of St. Charles were excellent seamstresses and were always making uniforms for one occasion or another and Erma's bridemaids' dresses were no different.

St. Charles, Texas was just like any other small town in Texas. It was segregated and accepted injustice. There was the fear of being lynched, constant oppression and much hopelessness. Life was just hard being born in the 1950's and growing up in the 1960's in East Texas. Cotton was still 'king' in Texas just like most towns in the U. S. Deep South. Summer was summer everywhere, but Texas was a different type of heat to work in each day. Most of the men worked in the cotton fields as sharecroppers and their mothers and wives took in wash for pay or were hired out as maids to clean houses or offices. People in St. Charles were accustomed to hard work, going to church and they stayed alive by keeping out of the way of the local authorities by following the written and unwritten rules of the town.

The young people attended Booker T. Washington Elementary with the one teacher for all grades, Ms. Tucker. School was open even during harvest time. It was a one room shack, clean and crowded with all of the students it could hold. Ms. Tucker was proud of her school and every student in it. Ms. Tucker made each student take pride in their school as well.

Ms. Tucker often said, "If this was the only place that the city will let us learn, we will take pride in ourselves and keep our school neat and clean." Ms. Tucker believed that education was a way out of poverty, sharecropping and being maids even if they were girls. All of the parents didn't agree with Ms. Tucker, but Ms. Tucker kept saying it in spite of the parents and society. Society was not on their side especially if you were female. Most girls' families believed that they should prepare themselves and look forward to marrying a nice man, raising children, living in a nice house and that was considered the good life.

Erma originally had four friends and they were called the fab five. Ida Mae had beautiful, smooth dark brown skin but, everyone called her Black Ida. She could fight and was strong against any boy in school. Frances was born breech and the mid-wife pulled her leg too hard which caused it to be bowed. Most people called her 'bowlegged Frances.' Frances' parents could not afford to get her legs fixed so she walked with a slight limp. Erma had teeth that protruded out of her mouth. Erma was able to close her mouth, but it wasn't easy.

Delores was naturally gorgeous. Her mother named her Delores but her dad always said she looked like Dorothy Dandridge. Ruby was red boned and light skinned with freckles and light reddish hair. Her family called her "red." As she got older she died her hair black so she would blend in but her natural hair color was red.

The kids at school and church picked on the Fab Five constantly. Being called by not so nice names gave them a complex, but because they had each other, the fab five kept going anyway. They believed that one day they would be blessed to live the abundant life that God had promised.

Ida Mae always kept them laughing, but she lied so much no one knew when she was actually telling the truth. She got plenty of whippings for her lying and Ida Mae was glad that she was dark skinned because it hid the scars. Frances kept them all dreaming of more and things outside of Texas. Frances loved clothes, was a great student and wore long skirts to hide her bowlegs. Delores was chased by all of the boys and men alike. They just couldn't get enough of how beautiful she was. Delores was tall with light brown skin, hazel eyes and long sandy brown hair. Delores was smart and kind to all.

Ruby just wished she didn't have those dots or freckles all over her face. The freckles wouldn't wash off and no makeup would cover them. Ruby tried once to cover the spots but got a whipping from her mother because she used too much of her mother's *Fashion Fair* foundation on her face. Erma was average height with medium brown skin, smart, kind and gentle to all but she had crooked teeth. Erma's parents didn't have the money to get her teeth fixed so she talked with her head down or her hand slightly raised to her face to hide her teeth. In the end, Erma just wanted to be loved and get her teeth fixed. Erma's parents weren't very loving. She didn't know her grandparents because they died before she was born so she didn't know how her parents were treated. Erma was a girl and the only hope for her to get out of this loveless house was to find a love of her own. She was a good child and didn't get many whippings like some children and especially not as many as Ruby and Ida Mae.

Parents in those days believed in whippings. You could get a whipping from your parents, someone else's parents or just an adult in school or at church. Good behavior was enforced.

The greatest relief from life was church. There was freedom at church. You could sing, clap your hands, scream, fellowship, dress up and be considered a human being in church. Erma and her four friends loved church. They sang in the sunshine choir, were junior ushers each fifth Sunday, on Saturdays, clean the church and anything else that needed to be done.

Sunday was always a time of worship, fellowship and a little rest from all of the hard work of the week.

"Erma!" Erma's mother called.

"Yes, ma'am?"

"Come in here and get your dress shoes on that your father shined last night." Her mother said sternly.

"Yes, ma'am."

Yes ma'am, no ma'am, yes sir and no sir was the majority of her conversation with her parents. Erma didn't spend time with her parents without a purpose, a task or duty. Erma pulled her Sunday dress over her head quickly and ran into the kitchen to get her Sunday black patent shoes that her dad shined with the big tub of Vaseline. It seemed that Vaseline could be used for everything including a moisturizer, shoe shiner, healing balm and lipstick or lip shine as her mother called it.

Once Erma put on her shoes and ran to her mother who was waiting on the front porch. Erma's father was already at church. He had been there much earlier to prepare for service. They had an older truck but it wasn't necessary to drive because they lived in a small house next to the church called the parsonage. The Smiths always arrived to church before anyone else. Erma helped her father with getting the church ready until her other four friends arrived.

Ida Mae was always the first to arrive. Ida Mae always came early to get out of her house. She walked alone to church which wasn't a good idea but she always said, "I can handle myself."

"Hey Ida Mae, how are you doing?" Erma asked when Ida Mae walked toward her. Ida Mae was in her usher uniform. The uniform was a black skirt and her one short sleeve white blouse.

"I'm fine. How are you Erma?" Ida Mae responded.

"Fine I guess." Erma said.

"You ready to usher this Sunday?" Ida Mae asked.

"Yes, there is your stack of fans on the end. I've got each of us the same number of fans to pass out during church," Erma said.

"Erma, look who is coming in now," Ida Mae asked. Erma was bent over straightening some of the fans that had fallen over on the seat. She didn't want any of the piles of fans to be uneven.

"Ida Mae, I can't guess and you might lie to me anyway. I don't trust you, let me look for myself." Erma said with her back still to the front door.

"Suit yourself."

Just then Erma heard footsteps on the wood floor coming closer and a voice said, "Hello Erma."

Erma turned at the voice too quickly and dropped all of the fans in her hand because she was so nervous. She could only get out, "Hey."

"Let me help you with that," Harold said as he bent down to help Erma pick up the fans. Harold Jamison was handsome with smooth brown skin that had been tanned by the sun, smart and kind. Erma had watched Harold several times from her bedroom window as he passed her house going to the store.

"Thank you so much," Erma said as she looked up over his head to a giggling Ida Mae. Erma just rolled her eyes.

"Here you go," Harold handed her the fans and walked away.

"Thanks," Erma said as she took the fans from his hand. He looked in Erma's eyes and winked so slightly.

When Harold walked away, Erma clinched her teeth and said, "Ida Mae can you ever be a friend and tell the truth! I didn't get to adjust my hair or dress or nothing before he walked up 'cause I can't trust you."

"I didn't lie Erma. I made a statement."

"Yes, you did." Erma was hot mad at Ida Mae. She didn't like to be teased or made fun of and especially, not by Ida Mae with those big white teeth just grinning.

Erma remembered Ida Mae saying, "Girl, look, there's a bug on you!"

The other girls would jump, scream or holler at the thought of a bug on them. Then Ida Mae would then smile with those big white teeth and say, "Ha, I made you look!"

She was lying all the time. There was no bug. No reason for alarm. In the end, the attention was on her and she had the last laugh.

One fifth Sunday while ushering, Ida Mae played a trick on Erma. She told Erma that Old Mother Robinson needed a fan. She walked to the front of church during the sermon and Old Mother Robinson already had a fan in her lap. She was scolded by her father for distracting him during the message and he almost lost his thought.

Delores came to church with her parents in a car. She had her uniform pressed and ready to usher. Frances and Ruby came in last. Their families lived the furthest away from church so they always arrived right before service started.

"Good morning ya'll," Erma said as they reached down to get their fans on the back seat.

"Good morning Erma. Good morning Ida Mae," Delores, Frances and Ruby said in unison. The five girls went outside to say a quick prayer and came back in to take their position in the four corners of the church. The older women in the church loved to see the younger women usher, sing or be in the pews. It was a way for them to learn responsibility, a love for God and a love for their church.

This Sunday there would be a church social after the service. Each family brought their dinner to church with them and they ate together outside on blankets. This would be time for fellowship and hopefully draw the attention of a nice young man.

At the end of service, Rev. Smith said the benediction and the blessing over the food and ended, "In thy darling son Jesus' name, Amen."

The entire church said a thunderous 'Amen.' Ms. Margaret Jones, who played for the church and the funeral home, began to play the familiar tune on the old stand up piano that was bought from the juke joint, 'God be with you until we meet again.' Women bent over and pulled their baskets and blankets from under their pews. The smell of chicken had been smelling throughout service. The men went to their cars and got the folding chairs and the coolers with the ice, lemonade and ice tea. The people filed out of the church family by family. The kids played tag, hide and seek or hopscotch until they were called to eat. Everyone shared what food that they had with the widows and visitors. There was always someone that came ill-prepared without enough plates, forks or a cup to drink something. The church members believed in sharing and no one going hungry.

Each mother kept an eye on their child as well as all of the other children in their area. Ida Mae's mother was always one that didn't bring enough. We all knew why because her father didn't work half of the time and there wasn't enough money for good and keep a roof over their heads.

"Ida Mae, sit with us and let me get you a plate," Erma said as she saw Ida Mae just standing off to herself not really joining in. Erma made sure to not hurt Ida Mae's pride.

"No, that's okay, I'll see what my mama brought," Ida Mae insisted.

"Well, go check out your mama's basket but you know I can't eat all of this. Share mine," Erma interjected.

"I will," Ida Mae said.

Delores, Frances and Ruby commented on Erma's hospitality.

"You are a great friend Erma," Delores said.

"I try to be. I know that her mom might not have brought enough food so I just wanted her to know that we had enough," Erma said.

"That's good," Frances replied.

"Here she comes back, hush," Ruby warned as Ida Mae approached them and sat on the blanket.

"What you got Erma?" Ida Mae asked as she sat down with only a biscuit and a piece of bologna on her plate.

"Plenty. Here you go," Erma passed her a bowl of potato salad, some sliced tomatoes and a plate of fried chicken. There was also a pound cake with caramel icing for dessert. Erma's mother was an excellent cook and always made enough for Erma to share with her friends.

"Thanks," Ida Mae said softly. The girls continued to eat, laugh and have fun. When they cleaned up their area, Erma pulled out her jacks, Delores had a deck of cards and Frances had her pick up sticks. Ida Mae brought no games with her but joined in anyway.

"Ida Mae go ahead and play with my jacks. I left my checkers in church. I'll be right back," Erma said as she leaped up and ran in church.

Erma ran into church and found the bag under the back seat. As she turned to leave out, there was a young man standing in the doorway. It was Ricky Jones, Ms. Margaret's son.

"Find what you are looking for?" Ricky was smiling and throwing a small red ball in the air.

Ricky Jones was always teasing Erma about one thing or another. Erma always felt uneasy around Ricky and she didn't know why.

"Yes, why?" Erma asked.

"Just checking. You know you are real pretty Erma."

"Thank you but I am headed back outside," Erma said as she tried to pass Ricky.

"You can't sit down and talk for just a minute?" Ricky smiled just so sweetly.

"Why do you want to talk to me? You are always making fun of me on the playground at school," Erma said.

"Well, have you ever heard that sometimes a man doesn't know how to say that he likes a woman so he just teases her?" Ricky asked again so smoothly.

"So are you saying you like me?" Erma asked.

"Yes, what do you think about that?" Ricky continued to press as he moved three steps closer.

"Well, I am not a grown woman and you are certainly not a grown man so I'll wait until I'm a grown woman to decide," Erma said.

"You got a smart mouth for a buck tooth girl."

"That's what I thought. You tried to be all nice 'cuz you want something from me. I don't know why you followed me in here. I don't have nothing for you. I'm gone," Erma tried to pass by Ricky to head out the door and he grabbed her by the arm.

"Get off of me. Let me go!" Erma exclaimed as she was hitting, scratching and trying to kick Ricky back. Ricky held on tightly but was soon grabbed and punched in the nose by Harold Jamison. Blood was on Ricky's white shirt and dripping down onto his black pants.

"What are you doing man?" Harold asked.

"I was just trying to be nice and then she slapped me," Ricky said as he held his bloody nose.

"That's a lie. All I said was I wasn't a grown woman and you wasn't a grown man and tried to walk away and he grabbed me," Erma explained.

"You liar and you will be an old maid forever," Ricky said.

"Get out of here before I hit you again," Harold said. Ricky left the sanctuary and ran the opposite way of the rest of the congregation still outside.

Harold turned to Erma, "You alright?" Harold had his hands on Erma's elbows trying to survey the damage. Erma was trying to pat down her hair and readjust her blouse and skirt. Erma may not have had a brother but Ida Mae had taught her a little about how to fight. Checkers were all over the floor and the checker board was under the pews two rows from the back.

"Yes, thank you for coming to my rescue. I never liked Ricky and don't know why he would do something like that," Erma was crying while picking up her checkers and putting them back in the bag.

"Don't cry Erma. All guys aren't like that. I'm sure not," Harold said as he helped Erma pick up her checkers.

When they both stood, Harold placed the checkers that he picked up into Erma's bag. She was still crying and he handed her his handkerchief.

"Here Erma, wipe your eyes," Harold insisted.

"Thank you again," Erma wiped her eyes and handed Harold his handkerchief back.

Unbeknownst to both of them, Ida Mae was standing outside the front door listening to it all.

She had come to see what was taking Erma so long to find the checkers. She saw Ricky coming out with a bloody nose and realized that there was an exciting tale waiting to be told and spread.

"Girl, guess what I just saw?"

"What Ida Mae? Don't lie, please don't lie."

"I'm going to tell the truth Delores. I promise. ."

"That's what you said the last time and it was a lie."

"No, really, I promise to God," Ida Mae said.

"Ida Mae don't go using the Lord's name in vain," Delores said.

"I'm not. Listen, I just saw Ricky run out of church with a bloody nose. Harold hit him because I think he was trying to do something to Erma. Erma's all cozy with Harold inside the church,"

"Ida Mae, you didn't go in there and check on her?" Ruby asked.

"No because it sounded like she was fine," Ida Mae smiled.

"Sounded like. You didn't see?' Delores asked.

"Was Harold still in there?" Ruby asked.

"Yep, he was. I don't know what was about to happen next but I came out here to tell ya'll," Ida Mae said.

"Come to spread rumors. Let's go ya'll and check on Erma before her parents find out," Frances beckoned.

All four girls ran inside the church door and found Erma sitting on the back pew and Harold sitting close to her. He was not touching Erma but they were talking quietly.

"You alright Erma?" Delores asked quietly.

Harold stood up from the pew and said, "Bye Erma," with a small wave of his hand just before he left the sanctuary.

Erma said, "Bye and thanks again Harold."

"Yeah, what happened?" Ruby asked as well.

"I saw blood on Ricky's shirt after Harold punched him," Ida Mae insisted.

"Shut up Ida Mae and let her tell it," Frances demanded.

"Okay," Ida Mae said. Her feelings were slightly hurt because she saw it all and should have been the one to tell.

"Well, I came in here to get my checkers and turned to leave, there was Ricky standing in the door way throwing a small red ball in the air. He said hi and asked if he could sit down and talk to me. I said, 'why do you want to talk to me?' He said, 'because sometimes a man likes a woman when he teases her.' I said, 'I'm not a grown woman yet and you're not a grown man.' He grabbed my arm and said I had a smart mouth for a bucked tooth girl and I started hitting him to make him let me go,"

"I taught you that Erma," Ida Mae said.

"Shut up, Ida Mae," Frances said.

"Stop telling me to shut up," Ida Mae insisted.

"Harold came in and pulled him off of me and punched him in the nose. I was crying and he handed me his handkerchief. Oh, I still have it. Harold helped me to pick up the checkers and find my board. We were sitting here talking when you guys came in. That's all,"

"Shucks, should we tell your parents?" Ruby asked.

"Nope don't mention it. He didn't do anything to me and I scratched him pretty good. Harold took care of the rest," Erma said with panic in her eyes.

"So Harold took care of the rest. I guess you are sweet on Harold," Ida Mae teased.

"Not really. I'm just thankful that's all," Erma said.

"You sure?" Ida Mae asked.

"Yes, I'm sure Ida Mae. Don't say nothing!" Erma yelled.

"I won't," Ida said.

"Ms. Margaret may stop playing for the church if she finds out. Then it will be my fault and I will get in trouble. Promise?" Erma pleaded.

"I promise."

They all went back outside and didn't mention the incident again. The basket supper was soon cleaned up and all of the members had gone home. Erma thought that the incident was over and her parents were none the wiser until a black belt came across Erma's back side and she leaped out of bed.

"Girl, what did you do to Ricky Jones in the sanctuary?" Erma's father demanded.

"Nothing sir I promise."

"What happened?"

"I went into the sanctuary to get my checkers and board under the back pew. He was standing at the doorway and said that he wanted to talk to me. He said that he liked me. He always teases me and the other girls on the playground at school. He said that men sometimes tease women instead of telling them they like them. I told him that I wasn't a grown woman and he wasn't a grown man. When I was a grown woman I would let him know," Erma said talking extremely fast.

"So you got smart with him?"

"Yes, but," Erma stopped because her father slapped her across the face so hard she fell to the floor.

"What happened next?" her father shouted.

Erma started to cry but she knew that she had to keep going. "Ricky grabbed my arm and I told him to let me go. I hit and kicked him but he still didn't let me go. Then Harold Jamison came in the door and punched Ricky in the nose and told Ricky to leave. That's all that happened. I promise."

"Ms. Margaret Jones said you lured her son into the church and wanted him to kiss you and then when he said no, you slapped him and then you punched him in the nose," Rev. Smith insisted.

"No, sir I didn't punch him in the nose. It was Harold Jamison. I'm sorry, but I didn't do anything sir I promise,"

"Harold Jamison! What was he doing in the church?" Rev. Smith asked.

"Father, he happened to walk by that is all! I didn't know he was anywhere around until he pulled Ricky off of me," Erma pleaded.

"You messing with Harold Jamison?"

"No, sir. I'm a good girl. I was just went to get my checkers. That is all! I promise," Erma insisted.

"Just stay away from all boys, you hear?"

"Yes sir," Erma muttered.

"Now, I have to go back to Old Mother Harris playing the piano because Ms. Margaret Jones quit because of you. If only I had a son, I wouldn't have to go through this mess." He left her room and slammed the door.

He finally said it. Her father wished she was a boy. Erma fell to the floor in tears until way in the night. She finally drug herself back to bed and cried herself to sleep. Her mother never came in to check on her and didn't speak to her the next day. It was Erma's fault that the church now had to have Old Mother Harris plunk on the piano instead of Ms. Margaret Jones playing.

That Sunday basket meeting changed everything. She told the truth and it still didn't matter. That same Sunday changed how Harold Jamison felt about Erma as well. He watched her every day at school and every Sunday at church. He didn't care that she had bucked teeth. She couldn't help that and maybe one day with enough money he would pay to fix her teeth. It was Erma's kindness, her body frame, her sweet brown face and bravery that attracted Erma to Harold. Harold dared Ricky Jones to come near Erma again even at school. He made sure to tell him.

As usual, Ida Mae overheard Harold threaten Ricky and ran to tell Erma and the other girls.

"What did you do to Harold Jamison, Erma?"

"Nothing, what do you mean?"

"You must have. I overheard Harold threaten Ricky Jones to not ever come near you again," Ida Mae teased.

"I don't know what you are talking about, but I will thank him the next time I see him," Erma said with a smile.

"I bet you will," Ida Mae teased.

"It's not like that! He's just nice to me," Erma shouted.

"Ida Mae, just leave Erma alone for once," Frances pleaded.

"I'll let you alone this time but I got my eyes open," Ida Mae warned.

Ruby and Delores just rolled their eyes and kept playing jacks on the playground. Erma's heart leaped on the inside but she kept a straight face. Ida Mae would never leave her alone if she really knew how she felt about Harold.

Two years later, Erma, Delores, Frances, Ruby, Ida Mae and Harold and the rest of the students of Booker T. Washington High School were all in the twelfth grade. It was the most important and activity filled year of school. There was Homecoming with the parade, the big game, the senior dance, award ceremony and then graduation. The girls spent hours at lunch discussing everything. What to wear? Who would be their date? What if this or that boy asked them to dance? What would they say or how they would act when he asked? Erma's only thought was, 'would her parents even let her go to the dance?'

Chapter 3

Harold was walking Erma home, carrying her books and made sure that no one teased her on the playground. Harold always handed Erma her books back by the time they got to the railroad tracks. He always stood at the corner in the grass and watched her until she was home.

Harold had just handed Erma her books just weeks before the dance.

"Bye Erma," Harold said walking backwards across the street looking directly at Erma.

"Bye Harold, see you tomorrow," Erma was waving goodbye to his smiling face. She had almost crossed the railroad tracks when a truck drove up beside her.

"Get in this truck girl!" It was her father. Erma didn't make it home in time before he got home from work. When her father pulled the truck into the driveway, he jumped out and yelled, "Get in the house now!"

Rev. Smith didn't care how loud he was or who heard him. As soon as Erma went in the front door, the black belt hit her from behind. Fortunately, he didn't hit her back, but it came across her behind. Her mother was in the kitchen and didn't even come out to see about Erma. Erma never knew how she got to age eighteen with so much neglect by her parents except when she was in trouble.

Unbeknownst to Erma, Harold was on the front porch and saw the whole thing. Harold grimaced every time Erma's father hit her. He could stand it no longer and knocked on the door.

"Rev. Smith, it's me Harold Jamison, please sir let me explain. It's not Erma's fault. It's my fault sir, please open the door and let me explain!" Harold pleaded through the door. Harold heard footsteps come across the hard wood floor but the door never opened.

"Boy go away from my front door or I will give you some of what Erma is getting. Yes, it's your fault and she's paying for it. Go away now," Rev. Smith instructed.

"But, sir..." Harold interrupted. He could hear quiet sobs from Erma but no screaming. Harold guessed she was just taking the whipping just like other kids. What could he do?

"But sir nothing. Go!" Rev. Smith returned to landing that black belt on Erma hind parts.

Harold remained at the door until it ended and then walked home sad. Harold wondered how would he ask Erma to the dance or ever marry her one day. The only thing Harold knew was that he loved Erma. Erma loved Harold too, he was sure of it. Harold was Erma's protector like the knights in shining armor in the books they read at school. .

The next day Erma walked to school as usual and Harold was nowhere in sight. She breathed a sigh of relief and sat down at her seat slowly because of her sore back side.

Frances was seated on the same wooden bench as Erma which were old church pews and asked, "You okay?"

"No," Erma said.

"What happened?"

"Father caught me walking home with Harold and I got the whipping of my life. What am I 'gonna do Frances?" Erma asked.

"I don't know but we have that math test today so pay attention to that. We'll figure out something at recess," Frances assured.

"Okay," Erma said sadly.

Harold passed Erma's end of the desk and whispered, "I'm sorry," while laying a red apple on it. Erma quickly, put the apple in her bag under the desk and got ready for the test.

On the playground later Erma said, "I don't know what to do. My parents are so mean. They won't let me do anything and I don't want another whipping because of Harold."

"I know it must be hard," Ruby said.

"I don't care what you say or how you tease me Ida Mae, I like Harold," Erma said sternly.

"I'm not going to tease you too much Erma. I like to play but whippings aren't fun and I've had my share of 'em. Sometimes they weren't even my fault," Ida Mae mused.

"I know what you mean. I told the truth and it still didn't make any difference," Erma said.

Harold walked up to the tree, "Can I talk to you Erma?"

"I don't think that it is a good idea Harold," Frances said.

"I know it's not a good idea Frances but I really have to talk to Erma. You girls can stay, I don't care," Harold never took his eyes off of Erma.

Erma said nothing. She just kept her head down and listened.

"I'm so sorry that you got a horrible whipping because of me. I tried to explain to your father but he wouldn't listen. I love you Erma. There I said it. I mean it too. I don't care how long it takes or what I have to do to convince your father but I will. I promise," Harold said and walked away.

Erma could not believe it. Harold loved her. The other girls couldn't believe it either. Each girl was a little envious of Harold's declaration to

Erma, but Ida Mae was full blown jealous. Ida Mae never heard the words of love spoken to her by anyone not even her parents. Ida Mae was just a body, work horse and the least of all, a girl. Delores knew that her parents loved her. They told her. Ruby and Frances' parents said that if they had a roof over their head and food to eat, that was love. Someone actually said that they loved Erma because five sets of ears heard it, along with God and all creation. Oh what a feeling!

Erma didn't know what to do. Old Mother Harris said that when you don't know what to do, just pray. So she prayed. Harold prayed too but he also stood under the tree across from Rev. Smith's house every day to try to talk to him. He tried to talk to him after church but Rev. Smith refused. Finally, Harold came to Rev. Smith's house with his parents. Mr. and Mrs. Jamison were kind people, attended church every week and loved their son completely. Mrs. Jamison had trouble having Harold so he was their only child, son and world.

Mr. Jamison knocked on the front door. Rev. Smith swung the door open with his back to the door and yelled, "Young man I said I'm not going to talk to you about my daughter!" Rev. Smith turned and realized that the Jamisons, faithful members, were standing at the door. "Excuse me. I didn't realize.."

"I know that you didn't realize, Rev. Smith. I find it rather difficult to understand why a man of the cloth would not take the time to listen to my son explain himself," Mr. Jamison said.

"Well, come in," Rev. Smith said sheepishly.

"Harold, stay on the porch," Mr. Jamison said. Harold sat down on the top porch step and waited. The Jamisons entered the living room and sat down on the couch.

"According to our son, he was walking your daughter home from school. He said he didn't get fresh with her by holding her hand or do anything out of the way. He told us that he was just walking her down the street carrying her books. Now, I understand that you have your own rules in your house Reverend but I am just trying to understand why you won't let my son be near your daughter?" Mr. Jamison asked.

"Well, you can imagine my concern about when young people get together things happen," Rev. Smith realized his reputation was on the line.

"We understand that too. But we have taught our son to respect women and not to take advantage of anyone even with his feelings. We've also taught him about the birds and bees. He is a normal eighteen year old and my wife and I think that it is important," Mr. Jamison continued.

"I understand. But you have to understand that we have a daughter and you have a son. My wife and I don't have the money or time to take care of out of wedlock kids," Rev. Smith explained.

"Who said that they would have children out of wedlock?"

"Well, I'm not talking about your son particular, but you know that things happen with young people today," Rev. Smith backtracked quickly.

"True but what if Mrs. Jamison and I were there anytime they would be alone? Would that be alright?" Mr. Jamison asked.

"Well, I guess. When would that be?"

"My son wants to take Erma to the Senior Dance. Would that be alright if we went sort of as a double date or does she have a date already?"

"Well, I guess so. Erma come in here!"

"Sir!" Erma said as she entered the room. Harold was no longer sitting on the porch but was sitting near and under the open window so he could better hear the conversation.

"Have you said yes to anybody else to go to the senior dance?"

"No sir!"

"Then the Jamisons want to know if you would go with their son Harold? They will accompany you both to the dance. Alright?"

"Yes sir." Erma said calmly. She tried to contain her excitement and didn't crack a smile, but returned to her room.

"Rev. Smith, like you, my wife and I want our child to be happy. Don't you agree?" Mr. Jamison asked.

"Of course. We all want what's best," Rev. Smith agreed.

"Well, we are going to leave you to your dinner and see you on Sunday. Goodbye," Mr. Jamison said as he held the door open for Mrs. Jamison to go out the front door.

Erma sat on the edge of her bed and wondered what just happened. One minute she was rubbing more liniment on her sore behind and trying to figure out if she would ever have a date. The next minute, the Jamisons had come in and convinced her father to allow them to escort her and Harold to the dance. When the Jamisons left, Erma's father called again.

"Erma come in here!"

Erma ran in the living room, "Yes, sir!"

"I am going to let you go to this dance with the Jamisons but if you embarrass me so help me you won't go anywhere else. You hear me?"

"Yes, sir," Erma said as she turned to go back to her room. It was settled.

Chapter 4

Harold obeyed his parents and made no attempt to be alone with Erma even at school. He didn't want anything to jeopardize the dance.

The weeks went by at school and the talk of the Senior Spring dance continued. Each girl had a new dress, shoes and a date except Ida Mae.

Even the bookworm, Abraham Johnson wouldn't go with Ida Mae. They tried every day to think of a boy that Ida Mae could go to the dance with. All of the boys said no. Ida Mae was bossy, teased incessantly and was mean to everyone. In the end, Ida Mae went alone wearing her Sunday dress and shoes.

The day of the spring dance Erma could hardly wait. She was so excited she couldn't eat because Ms. Marie had made the soft green dress to fit Erma perfectly. The Jamisons arrived at 5:00

p.m. just as they promised. When Erma saw Harold looking so handsome she couldn't help but blush. Harold wore a brown suit, a white shirt and his father's favorite tie with a lapel pin that had his father's initials. Harold was all smiles as he presented Erma a red rose corsage that complimented her dress perfectly. The dance was to be held at the juke joint or the local club because it was the only place in St. Charles that black people could rent out for an event besides the church or someone's barn. To make sure that the juke joint didn't lose any money on a Saturday night, the dance was to start at 5:30 p.m. and end by 8:30 p.m. The other classmates arrived to the dance in their finest including Ida Mae. The girls took a picture together along with their dates. They put Ida Mae in the middle of the group to somehow not bring attention that she had no date. The night was going smoothly. Erma danced with Harold. Harold danced with his mother and Harold's father danced with Erma. Erma almost cried when Harold's father asked her to dance. She would have loved for her own father and mother to have been there but they were home in their own little world. After Harold danced with his mother, she got tired and sat down. Harold took this chance to go outside to the outhouse because there was no inside plumping at the juke joint. The outhouse was located behind the juke joint only a short ways from the back door yet it was far enough for privacy. When Harold slammed the rickety outhouse door, Ida Mae approached.

"Hello Harold," Ida Mae purred. Harold stopped short at the mention of his name.

"Hello Ida Mae. What do you want?" Harold asked as he kept walking but Ida Mae stopped him short by getting in front of him and putting her finger in his chest.

"Well, I'm just wondering what is really so special about Harold Jamison? Erma seems to be so taken with you," Ida Mae said as she batted her eyes and puckered her lips like her mama taught her.

"I don't know what you mean?" Harold asked as he tried to move past her but she blocked him again with her body.

"Well, it's the last dance of the school year and you have only danced with Erma and your mama. So I was wondering if you would dance or something else with me."

"You know I am not going to dance with or anything else with you, Ida Mae. I love Erma," Harold said firmly.

"Well, it looks like I'm just going to have to take what I want," Ida Mae said as she grabbed Harold by his shirt collar and kissed him on the mouth. Ida Mae was as strong as any man Harold knew.

Harold had always been taught not to hit girls but he had to get away from her and quick before someone saw him. He placed his hands on Ida Mae's shoulders and gave her a firm push just enough to get her off of him. Instead of getting away from her, Ida Mae brought him closer in her grasp.

"Get off of me. What are you doing?" Harold said.

"Taking what I want and now I've got proof," Ida Mae grabbed the tie off of Harold shirt because it was on a clip on tie, it came off easily. On the other hand, the tie pin was attached to his shirt. The force of Ida Mae pulling the tie and tie pin, it tore Harold's shirt. Ida Mae took off running because she was the fastest girl in school. Harold started to run after her but stopped in his tracks. How would he explain the torn shirt and no tie? He closed his suit jacket and went back inside. When Harold came in the door, he knew that it was all over. He saw Ida Mae along with Erma,

Delores, Frances and Ruby in the back corner. He knew that she was telling her side of the story. Harold walked to his parents.

"Mom and Dad, it's time to go," Harold said with his head down.

"Why are you ready to go and where is your tie and my tie pin?" Mr. Jamison asked.

"I'll explain in the car," Harold walked to the door and then to the car.

"We can't go anywhere without Erma. She is with her friends. I'll let her know that we are ready to go," Ms. Jamison said. She walked over to the girls and overheard the conversation.

"He don't really love you Erma. I've got his tie and the tie pin,"

"How did you get that Ida Mae?" Frances asked.

"Harold tried something outside at the outhouse. I was coming out of the outhouse first and he saw me before he went in and asked for a kiss. I told him no but he kissed me anyway. In the struggle.." Ida Mae said with a smile.

"Struggle? Why was there a struggle?" Ruby asked.

"Well, you girls don't know how real kissing is. Sometimes there is a little struggle between a man and a woman," Ida Mae said grinning.

Erma just ran off in tears right past Ms. Jamison. Ms. Jamison hurried after Erma along with Frances.

"You are terrible Ida Mae," Delores said as she ran after Erma and Frances.

"Ruby, you believe me don't you?" Ida Mae asked.

"Nope, I don't believe you either. You are rotten Ida Mae and you will reap what you have sown. Erma has been a real friend to you when you didn't deserve it. You had no right to do that to Erma or Harold. They don't deserve that. You are horrible," Ruby walked away as well. Ida

Mae stood there with the evidence but at what price.

Mrs. Jamison walked back into the dance and approached Ida Mae, "Ida Mae give me that tie and tie pin. I should whoop you myself but you're not worth it. I dare you to come near my son again do you hear me?" Ida Mae handed it to her. She should be ashamed but was she?

Ida Mae had ruined the dance for everyone. Harold was standing outside of the car waiting on his mother and Erma. Harold's father opened the back door of the car for Erma and waited for his wife to come out of the juke joint and join her. Erma just looked out the window in silence with tears still running down her face. Harold opened the passenger side of the car, sat down and slid forward in his seat. Harold, Jr.'s elbow was on the car door and his head was in his hands. He just wanted this night to be over.

"Okay before we start this car, Erma, I am so sorry about what happened tonight at the dance. I don't know exactly what happened but I want Harold to explain," Mr. Jamison said.

"That's okay, Mr. Jamison, you can just take me home," Erma said quietly.

"No, you deserve an explanation and so do we. Go ahead Harold," Mr. Jamison said. Harold turned in his seat to face Erma.

"I was coming out of the outhouse after handling my business. Ida Mae came from behind the outhouse and surprised me. She asked what was so special about me. I told her I didn't know what she meant. She said that she wanted me to dance with her or something else. I told her that I loved you Erma and I didn't want to dance with her or anything else. She then grabbed me by my tie, pulling me toward her and kissed me on the lips. I placed my hands on her shoulders to push her away. Instead, she grabbed my tie and the tie pin so hard that she tore my shirt. That is it Erma I promise. I sit here before God and my parents and tell you that I love you for real," Harold pleaded.

"That's fine Harold. Right now, I don't know what to believe and I just want to go home," Erma said quietly. Mr. Jamison felt sorry for Erma and his son. Jealousy is a terrible thing and can hurt a lot of people. Mrs. Jamison's heart hurt for both of these young people. They were still young and hopefully, would get past it. Mr. Jamison started the car and they all rode in silence to Erma's house. Erma jumped out of the car quickly after saying goodbye and thanking the Jamisons again for taking her to the dance. Erma ran into the house to silence and the kitchen stove light on to guide her to her bedroom. In her bedroom, she took off her new dress and cried herself to sleep without a word from her parents.

Chapter 5

The next day was Sunday. Erma was carrying out her duties but with no energy because her heart was broken. Erma sat on the back seat with the ushers and just sulked. The Jamisons along with Harold walked by and waved at Erma but said nothing. Harold turned around during the hymn singing to try to get her attention but Erma kept her head down in the hymnal the entire time. At the end of service, Frances walked up to Erma. "You alright?" Frances asked.

"No, I feel terrible," Erma said sadly.

"I know. Ida Mae is a mean person," Frances stated.

"Yes and that was the final dance of our school days too. Why would she do that Frances?" Erma pleaded.

"Green eyed monster of jealousy Erma. It's no excuse but she gets pleasure out of teasing and hurting others. It's because she is so miserable herself. She didn't have a date, new dress or shoes to the dance so she decided to ruin your time at the dance," Frances said.

"I guess so but I have been a good friend to Ida Mae. I thought Harold really cared about me too," Erma said.

"He does. I almost forgot. Take this," Frances handed Erma a note.

Erma unfolded the small sheet of paper and read, 'I am so sorry. I really love you Erma. Harold.' Erma wanted to tear up the paper and throw it in Harold's face but she just put the note in her pocket.

"Thanks Frances," Erma said.

"You are welcome. Talk to you at school on Monday. Bye Erma," Frances said.

"Bye," Erma walked out the side door of the church to her house next door. Erma knew that she would see Ida Mae and Harold at school on Monday as well. School would only meet for half days for seniors because they were taking their final exams.

Erma and her parents ate their Sunday dinner in silence. Erma asked, "May I be excused to my room?"

"Yes," her father said.

Erma washed her plate, utensils and glass in the sink. After drying each item, she put them away in the cupboard. She went immediately to her room, got out her books and spread them on her bed. She raised her window for some fresh air and began studying Math which was her hardest subject. She heard footsteps on the porch and looked out to see Ricky Jones standing at the front door.

'What does Ricky Jones want?' Erma thought with a panic. She hadn't danced with him, seen him or talked to him since that Sunday she got that horrible whipping. She closed her book and listened at the window.

Rev. Smith went to the front door, "Yes Ricky, what can I do for you?" Rev. Smith asked politely.

"Can I see Erma please?"

"Why do you need to see Erma?"

"I just need to tell her something sir. It's important. You can stay on the porch and hear everything. It is nothing that Erma did I promise," Ricky pleaded.

"Erma! Come to the door," Rev. Smith yelled.

Erma came to the front door, "Yes sir,"

"Ricky Jones has something to tell you," Rev. Smith said with a frown.

Erma walked out onto the front porch and said nothing. Rev. Smith stood in the doorway with the screen door closed to not let in flies but to hear the entire conversation. Mrs. Smith was close by as well.

"Erma first let me say that I have been a horrible person to you because I got you in trouble by lying about you getting fresh with me. It was my fault Rev. Smith. Second, I saw everything between Harold and Ida Mae. I was being bad as always smoking a cigarette with members of the band at the dance. I was behind the juke joint and saw everything. I swear to God I am telling the truth,"

"No need to swear, son just tell the truth," Rev. Smith said. Erma wondered why her father called him, 'son' but wouldn't treat her like his real daughter?

"I'm sorry Rev. Smith. I promise, I am telling to the truth. Harold came out of the outhouse and

Ida Mae was behind the outhouse and came up to him. She put her finger in his chest and stopped him. I couldn't hear what she was saying but the next thing I knew, she was pulling him by his jacket and kissed him on the mouth. He took her by the shoulders and pushed her off of him. Ida Mae grabbed his tie and it popped right off because she pulled so hard, his shirt tore where the tie pin was attached. She ran away from him with the tie in her hand and he started to go after her but stayed to fix his clothes instead. It was Ida Mae, Erma. All Ida Mae. I swear, I mean, I promise," Ricky said eagerly.

"We believe you Ricky. Have a safe journey home," Rev. Smith said backing away from the doorway.

"Thank you for telling me," Erma said quietly and went back into the house.

"I didn't know anything bad happened at the dance Erma," Rev. Smith said.

"It doesn't matter," Erma said quietly and looked at her father. Her father's concern was more than Erma could bear. Her father believed Ricky over' her. Mrs. Smith overheard the entire conversation but never once asked Erma about it, even after Ricky left.

Erma went into her bedroom, closing the door and cried again. Harold really did care about her and Ida Mae really was that horrible. Erma laid across her bed only a short time to return to studying her math. For now, the truth was enough.

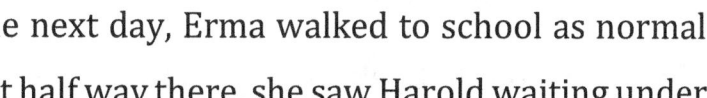

The next day, Erma walked to school as normal but half way there, she saw Harold waiting under the big oak tree.

"Erma, can I talk to you?" Harold asked as Erma got within shouting distance of their tree.

"Yes," Erma replied.

"I didn't kiss Ida Mae. Ida Mae grabbed and kissed me," Harold explained.

"I know," Erma said.

"Believe me. I don't even like Ida Mae. Wait. You know? How do you know?" Harold asked.

"Ricky Jones came by our house yesterday and told me and my father the whole story. What you don't know is that Ricky saw the whole thing. He swore and promised to God that he was finally for once in his life telling the truth," Erma said and laughed.

"You believe him?" Harold asked.

"Yes," Erma said with a smile.

"But, you wouldn't believe me?" Harold pressed.

"No, it wasn't that I didn't believe you. I wanted to believe you but she was standing there with your father's tie with the tie pin still on it. What do you think I would think?"

"You have a point," Harold agreed.

"That's what Ida Mae was hoping for when she grabbed your tie. She wanted it as proof," Erma said.

"You're right," Harold said.

"By the way, we have to get to school before we are late for our exams. You ready?" Erma asked.

"For exams? As much as I could be while worried about whether you were going to believe me or not,"

"Well, I believe you and math is your best subject so you should do well," Erma said.

"Yeah, I guess. Let's go," Harold said and took off toward school. Erma was running and laughing trying to keep up. They arrived at school right on time and took their exams with no problems. At recess, Erma. Ruby, Frances and Delores were sitting under the tree eating their lunch. Ida Mae approached them.

"Hey everybody," Ida Mae said.

No one responded not even Ruby. "I'm really sorry Erma. Harold just came up to me and kissed me. I don't know why," Ida Mae said.

"You are lying again Ida Mae," Erma said.

"Just stop it," Frances added.

"We all know the truth," Delores concurred.

"Tell the truth for once," Ruby said.

"No, I am not lying. It happened just like I said!" Ida Mae exclaimed.

"No it did not! Ricky Jones saw everything and came to our house yesterday and told me the truth. His story is the same as Harold's," Erma screamed.

"You believe Ricky Jones and Harold over me?" Ida Mae asked.

"Yes," the four said in unison.

"You kicking me out of the fab five?" Ida Mae inquired.

"You kicked yourself out. How can I trust you any more, Ida Mae? You went too far this time," Erma said.

Ida Mae had nothing else to say so she just walked away. The fab five now became the fab four.

Julia Royston

Chapter 6

The school year ended with the graduation of the class of 1968 and the world was in turmoil. Martin Luther King, Jr. and Senator Robert Kennedy were assassinated. The U. S. was at war in Vietnam and the hopes of marrying a wonderful man, having children and building the abundant life were dim and slim.

God smiled on the young women from St. Charles, Texas. Delores moved to Atlanta and attended the famed Spelman College. Frances and Ruby moved to Houston to attend Texas Southern. Erma's parents allowed her to attend Wiley College to obtain a 2 year administrative degree. Ida Mae stayed home to care for her family.

Harold went to the oil fields. It was the hardest work of his life. His parents wanted him to go to college but he was great with his hands and wanted money enough to get a house, car and insurance for Erma. He wanted to prove his love for Erma. At Erma's graduation from Wiley, Harold showed up with a ring. He got down on one knee and proposed before her parents, his parents and Erma's entire graduating class. Harold had received permission from her father and in spite of all of Rev. Smith's objections, Harold loved and wanted to marry Erma more today than ever before.

Harold moved Erma to a Houston small shot gun house with 3 bedrooms, a small kitchen and a small living room/family room, but it was theirs. Harold loved Erma in every way. He was Erma's best friend, confidante, husband, protector and lover. Harold made Erma feel things and see things that she never dreamed possible. Erma's heart almost burst with love and pride in what Harold's love did for her self-esteem and outlook on life. Their love produced three children in the first 5 years of marriage. Erma didn't care how busy she was because her heart was large enough for her four loves, Harold and her three children, Harold, Jr., Harriett and Edith Jamison. She was finally happy. Harold was a man of his word and kept his promise. In between bearing children, Erma was finally able to get her teeth repaired with the dental insurance that Harold worked so hard to pay for. Harold said that she was beautiful no matter what but he knew that with her teeth repaired she would be more confident. Harold always encouraged Erma to use her degree in any way possible at church or in the community. He said that the children would grow up and her degree would come in handy one day.

Two years later, those words came true. A police officer and a supervisor of the oil company rang their doorbell.

"Harold, Jr. get the door," Erma yelled as she cut the stove down from boil and checked the bread in the oven. Harold, Sr. would be home soon and then they would eat dinner. Harold, Jr. ran to the front door and opened it just slightly.

"Hello, can I help you?" Harold, Jr. said in mature voice for a seven year old.

"Yes, is your mother home?"

"Yes, she is," Harold, Jr. said as he ran to the kitchen to get his mother. "Mama, there are two white men at the front door for you."

"Shh, Harold, Jr., that's not nice to say. Let me go see what they want," Erma wiped her hands on her apron and walked to the door.

"Can I help you sir?" Erma asked as she opened the front door wider.

"Mrs. Jamison?" the policer officer asked.

"Yes," Erma asked politely.

"I'm sorry to have to notify you ma'am but there has been a terrible accident at the East Houston Oil Company. Your husband, Mr. Harold Jamison has been killed by the explosion," the company representative.

"No!" Erma screamed and passed out on the floor. The Jamison's next door neighbor, Mrs. Lewis, a white older lady, came running at the scream and ran onto the porch. Mrs. Lewis only saw two white men bent over her Negro neighbor and she could only think the worst.

"Leave them alone. They are great colored neighbors. They don't bother nobody. Don't hurt Erma, please!"

"Excuse me ma'am," the police officer said, "We are not hurting her. We came to tell her that her husband was killed in an accident and she fainted."

"Oh my Lord, that is awful," Mrs. Lewis cried.

The police officer and company representative left the paper work and the box of Harold Jamison's personal effects that were retrieved from his locker with Mrs. Lewis. When Erma came to, the children were fed, in their beds asleep and she was laying on the couch with a cold compress on her head. Mrs. Lewis had left the children alone for only 2 minutes to turn the stove off so the food wouldn't burn. Mrs. Lewis lived alone so she felt it was her Christian duty to help Erma during this very difficult time. Mrs. Lewis finished the dinner, put the dishes in the sink, put the kids to bed and waited until Erma could finally get herself together.

"Oh Mrs. Lewis, thank you so much for all of your help," Erma said.

"You are fine child. I don't have nobody else to take care of so I guess Jesus means for me to help you today. I'm so sorry Erma," Mrs. Lewis said sadly.

"Me too. I don't know what I am going to do now," Erma said.

"Right now, you are going to lock the door behind me when I leave out. There is a plate in the oven if you feel like eating. You should eat because you are going to need your strength. After that, you are going to go to your bedroom, get in the bed and rest. You don't have to make any decisions right at this moment. Tomorrow will be here soon enough," Mrs. Lewis replied.

Erma got up from the couch slowly to let Mrs. Lewis out and lock the door. Once the door closed, she fell to the floor again. What was Erma to do?

The next day Erma faced her children with the news of their father's passing. It was hard for them and even harder for Erma. The girls screamed and little Harold ran outside and climbed a tree. They all cried for what seemed like hours. Harold, Jr. remembered his father always said, "Little Harold when I'm gone to work, you are the man of the house." This was never more true than today.

Erma sat on the couch with the girl's arms wrapped around her as tight as possible. She wanted to check on Harold, Jr. but from the couch she could see that he was just rocking back and forth in the tree. She decided to let him be for now. The children were seven, six and five years old and now without a father. No fault of their own. No lack of love and respect between their parents. No divorce. No cheating. No abuse, just love. Death had come and snatched the head of the house, their role model, their protector, father and Erma's first true love. All was quiet in the house. Little Harold finally came back in the house to sit on the couch with his sisters. They sat there staring out into nothing but the blue wallpaper that Harold and Erma fussed and teased each other about for hours.

Erma went into her bedroom, sat down and first called her parents. Her father said how sorry he was but didn't offer to pay for anything, come for the funeral or speak at the service. Erma's mother didn't even speak to her over the phone. Nothing but sorry. Erma and Harold were faithful to the small Baptist church down the street. They loved the weekly walks hand in hand with strollers to church. Erma guessed that she would have the service there.

Erma's next call was to the Jamisons. In Erma's heart, they were now her parents because they had always treated her like a daughter. Mrs. Jamison answered the phone, "Hello."

"Mother Jamison?" Erma said quietly.

"Hey baby, why is your voice so low? What's the matter?" Mrs. Jamison asked.

"Mother Jamison, Harold was killed yesterday at work." Erma said quietly.

"What did you say?" Mrs. Jamison asked again.

"He's gone, Mother Jamison. My husband is gone!" Erma cried.

"Not my baby! He's all I had! No God no!!" Mrs. Jamison screamed, then there was a thud on the floor.

Erma cried as she yelled into the phone, "Mother Jamison, I'm so sorry! I didn't know how else to tell you. I'm so sorry. Mother Jamison are you alright?" Erma heard heavy feet running and Father Jamison yelling, then the scrape of the phone on the hard wood floor and then a familiar voice.

"Hello! Erma what happened? What happened?" Mr. Jamison yelled into the phone.

"Oh Father Jamison it's awful. They came to the house yesterday and said that there was an explosion and Harold was killed. They dropped off a box of his things from his locker and that was it. My husband is gone! I am left alone with my three babies!" Erma cried.

"I'm so sorry for you, my grandbabies and for me. God knows I loved my boy. He was all we had. He made me so proud. We are on the way as soon as we can get together," Mr. Jamison said between gulps of tears.

"Be careful and thank you for everything. I can't wait to see you both," Erma said as she hung up the phone, fell back on the bed and yelled out, "God help me!!"

The children ran into the bedroom with Erma and the four of them just laid on the bed staring up at the ceiling as Erma's tears subsided and they all fell asleep.

Julia Royston

Chapter 7

Two days later with every ounce of strength they could muster, the Jamisons arrived in Houston to stay as long as it took to stabilize their daughter in law and grandchildren. Mrs. Jamison was still numb at the thought of losing her only child. She had prayed so long and hard for a son and God granted that request, but now he is gone.

They all stood near the front door in a group embrace for a long time. The children were a great comfort to the Jamisons despite the devastating loss of their son. Erma wondered if she would lose her mind, but she didn't. In spite of the difficulties, Erma held it together for her three babies and Harold's parents.

The following day, Mr. Jamison went to the bank with Erma to discuss her financial situation. Harold, Jr. and Erma had been very frugal with their money and had a nice savings. When Erma went through Harold's personal effects, she found another insurance policy in the case of his death, dismemberment or accident. The policy was in his work locker and in the amount of $15,000. Two days later, two more gentlemen from the oil company showed up again. This time, they had a check for $10,000 for accident insurance. Erma knew of another insurance policy that they had kept on both of them in case of their death. This policy was in the amount of $50,000. If one of them died, they would receive half of the policy amount, which was $25,000. Erma had a total of $50,000 of insurance money to invest, pay off bills or pay off the house. The Jamisons paid six months of the mortgage in advance to ensure that they would have a place to live until Erma got a job. It was now time to put that two year degree to good use.

Erma's parents arrived one day before the funeral. They stayed in a hotel because they felt it was too crowded in Erma's small house. Erma was prepared for her parents to stay in the girl's bedroom, but it didn't happen. Erma's parents hardly knew their grandchildren. Secretly, Erma didn't want her children around her parents because of their cold and non-caring attitude. Her children didn't deserve that now more than ever. Erma had too much on her plate to care about her parents' behavior.

While the ladies were cleaning up the kitchen after dinner, Mr. Jamison asked Rev. Smith if he would take a walk with him. They walked in silence until they arrived at a small park.

Once inside the park, they both sat down on a bench. Mr. Jamison asked, "So what's the real problem Sam?"

"What do you mean?" Rev. Smith asked.

"You are supposed to be a man of the cloth, a minister of the gospel of Jesus Christ's love and you are about as loving as a rattle snake!" Mr. Jamison exclaimed.

"I can't help it. I can't show something I've never seen. I was never loved. I was beaten night and day by a crazy mother and horrible step-father. I still have the scars on my back. I don't know what love looks like. My wife was pregnant before Erma and it was a boy. He only lived a week! I always wanted a boy. I lost a son and then I had a daughter. Sure she is a wonderful, smart young lady, but how can my name go on with a girl?"

"I lost a son too! My boy was burned to death and I don't even have a body to bury tomorrow! I will have my boy in my mind and in my heart forever. My boy is gone but I love my wife and she is still here. I love my daughter in law and I sure as hell love my grandbabies!" Mr. Jamison yelled.

"Yes, and that grandson has your name! I don't have that!" Rev. Smith yelled.

"What does that have to do with loving someone? That's selfishness. You are making this about you and not your child. Your daughter has your blood running through her veins. That should be enough to show love, care and concern. You are making an excuse. You don't have love because you don't want it. Jesus can put enough love in your heart to erase all of the pain you had from childhood. You must like the hurt and pain because you keep reliving it and holding on to it. I hurt right now for my boy. It will take me a while but I'll get through it because I know that I loved my boy with everything in me and my boy loved me too. My boy loved his mama and his mama loved him back. If you and your wife don't find any love in those cold, scarred and angry hearts, you will have lost not only a son but a daughter and three beautiful grandchildren. I have no respect for someone who can't move beyond their family upbringing. Whoever heard of such? All of that preaching about God, Jesus and His love and you didn't get none of it. They didn't teach you nothing at that Bible College just a bunch of words on paper but nothing got down in your heart. Well, don't worry, I have enough love, care and protection in me for them all. Think about that Reverend Sam Smith," Mr. Jamison said as he walked quickly down the road back to the house.

Rev. Smith stayed sitting on that bench and just cried. They were slow, hot, salty, silent tears of regret and longing for the love he never had and his refusal to learn how to show and share.

The next day the memorial service was held at the Baptist church down the street. Mr. Jamison insisted that they go in the car instead of walking and the Smiths followed in their car. Since there were no bodily remains there was a picture of Harold Jamison, Jr. on a stand on the table at the altar. The new, young minister who preached the sermon was Robert H. Carter. He was originally from Atlanta and had recently graduated from Morehouse College's Cozer Theological Seminary where the famous Dr. Martin Luther King, Jr. attended. Robert Carter moved to Houston only six months before Harold's death and was given the task of preaching this young father's funeral. The words were all in order, he didn't preach long and the service was beautiful. The church provided a repass of wonderful food after the service in the basement of the church since there was no need to go to the cemetery. The children went outside to play in the fenced yard of the church until the adults were ready to go home. Erma sat on the back steps keeping a close eye on her children. Surprisingly, Robert Carter was throwing a ball to little Harold and the girls were running back and forth playing tag. Erma wiped a tear knowing that little Harold wouldn't be able to throw the ball to his dad. Erma made a promise to herself that with God's help she would work hard to provide the life that both she and Harold dreamed about.

"Come on children, I think it's about time for us to go," Erma said while standing on the steps.

"Yes, mama," the girls said in unison.

"Thanks Rev. Carter for throwing me the ball," little Harold said.

"Sure, Harold anytime. I played baseball on my college team and anytime your mom says, I'd be happy to work with you on your baseball skills," Rev. Carter said as they walked closer to Erma. The three children went inside of the building and Erma stopped Rev. Carter.

"Thanks Rev. Carter. I really appreciate you taking the time with little Harold. I think it is going to be hardest on him than even the girls," Erma explained.

"No problem. It will be hard on you all and not just little Harold. I lost my father around his age and I know what that is like. It is hard but you get through it. I had a great step father who helped me. I made it and so will he. Anything I can do, let me know," Rev. Carter said.

"Thanks so much. The service was wonderful and your sermon was encouraging," Erma added.

"I am glad," Rev. Carter said as he watched Erma turn and climb the few steps to get inside of the church. He knew that she was carrying the weight of the world on your shoulders. He watched his mother do it when his father died. She was now at the top of his prayer list.

Erma's parents left the next morning early. It was Saturday so the Smiths had to get home to prepare for Sunday morning service. The Jamisons promised to help Erma with whatever they needed as long as they needed it.

When the Jamisons left, Erma learned to get through the day by herself with the children. Her neighbors looked out for her too, but Erma believed that she should manage her household on her own and with God's help, she would.

Chapter 8

After three months, it was time for Erma to find a job. She started looking in the newspapers for administrative and clerical jobs but some were too far from the house. Others didn't pay enough for child care, gas to and from the job or there were too many buses to catch and still get the kids to school on time so Erma kept looking.

On Sunday morning, Rev. Carter announced that Mrs. Montgomery would be retiring as the church secretary and clerk after 40 years. There would be a retirement celebration the next Sunday immediately after service. In the meantime, they would be looking for applicants and if qualified, please apply. Erma thought, this would be perfect. The church was in the neighborhood and only a few blocks from the children's school. She had worked for years with her father at his church in St. Charles and she did have her administrative degree. She would apply. When Erma approached Rev. Carter after service, to ask about the position, she was not the only one interested. Because Rev. Carter was single, there were several young women standing at the altar to ask him about the job. Erma was interested in the job and not Rev. Carter. Erma decided to ask Rev. Carter about the job later and turned to walk out the front door. Little Harold got away from her and ran up to Rev. Carter to speak. Little Harold said, 'excuse' leaving out 'me' and pushed past the ladies waiting to say hello.

"Hello Rev. Carter," Little Harold said boldly.

"Hello little Harold. Give me five," Rev. Carter said as he held his hand out for little Harold to slap it soundly. "That's it! How have you been doing?" Rev. Carter asked knowing that he probably was missing his father in a house filled with females.

"Fine but I want to throw a ball with you again some time," little Harold said proudly.

"Sure, let your mom know and you all can come by anytime that you see my car here. I always have my baseball in my desk drawer and we can play catch whenever. Uh oh, here comes your mother," Rev. Carter said as he looked up to see Erma coming down the aisle somewhat perturbed.

"Yes, sir. I think I'm in trouble. Bye Rev. Carter," little Harold said sadly when he also saw his mother's face.

Erma came toward Rev. Carter, "I'm sorry and I hope little Harold wasn't bothering you. Excuse me sisters," Erma said as she reached for little Harold's hand through the group of women and the smell of the alluring perfumes almost made Erma sneeze.

"He's alright Sis. Erma. He just wanted to speak. He's fine. Bye Harold," Rev. Carter said never taking his eyes off of Erma. There was just something about this woman that drew him to her.

"Bye Rev. Carter," little Harold said looking back one more time. Rev. Carter watched Erma, little Harold and the girls until they left out the front door of the church. He knew that sad look in little Harold's eyes. He knew that worried look around Erma's mouth and eyes as well. He had seen it on his mama's face. He knew that his stepfather had taken that look off of his mother's face and prayed that one day someone would take that sad, worried look off of Erma's face.

Rev. Carter went back to talking with the group of women he hoped would be interested in the secretary position and not just in him.

Meanwhile, Erma was walking and talking about little Harold's actions.

"Little Harold did you say excuse me when you walked up on grown people's conversation?"

"Yes ma'am."

"I hope so because your father and I are, I mean, I am trying to raise smart, respectable children and not ones with no home training. Do you hear me?" Erma almost choked when she heard herself say, your father and I. Everything had changed.

"But, Rev. Carter said that we could come by any time that we saw his car and he would throw his baseball with me. Please mama, can we?" little Harold pleaded.

Erma felt like sitting down on the pavement and crying at the sound of little Harold's plea. She knew it was a combination of missing his father, being the only male in the house and those little league baseball tryouts posted at the school. How could Erma resist?

Erma said instead, "We shall see." Erma didn't want to get little Harold's hopes up but what Erma had seen of Rev. Carter so far, he was a man of his word.

The weeks following the funeral consisted of school, cleaning up the house and bedtime each night. The Jamisons called every other day to check on them and spoke to each child about how they were doing and their days at school. 'What a phone bill they are running up,' Erma thought but she was appreciative. After Harold's death, her parents maintained their distance and sadly enough, that was to be expected.

At 3:45 on Wednesday, Erma walked the short distance to her children's school and then returned home. Every day was the same, the children ran and hugged her when they saw her waiting for them on the sidewalk.

She asked each one how their day was at school, what they ate for lunch and were there any problems. Each one had a good day but little Harold knew that it was Wednesday and bible study night.

"Mama can we go to the church a little early so I can throw Rev. Carter's baseball with him?" little Harold asked.

"We'll see, little Harold. We have to eat, clean up the kitchen and get ready quickly. Church starts at 6:30 and we don't want to bother Rev. Carter," Erma said.

"But, Rev. Carter said," little Harold insisted.

"I know what Rev. Carter said but we shall see what happens when we get to church. He may only have a few minutes." Erma said.

"It doesn't matter how long I just want to learn to throw the baseball so I can make the team," little Harold said with a smile.

The children picked up their walking pace led by little Harold and Erma had to smile at their excitement. The girls could always find ways to play whether it was tag, hop scotch or running after butterflies. It was spring, sunny and always hot in Texas. The children ran into the house, changed from their school clothes to church clothes. The girls had no homework but little Harold sat down on the couch to finish up his math. The girls put the plates on the table as Erma dished up the food. It was little Harold's turn to say grace and he didn't waste any time doing it.

"Good bread, good meat, thank you God and let's eat," was all little Harold had to say.

Erma smiled as they all said, 'Amen.'

Erma still left the head of the table chair empty. The girls still sat on one side, little Harold sat on the opposite side, Erma sat in the chair facing that empty chair where once sat the love of her life. Lord, how would she go on without him? Only the Lord gave her strength each day. Little Harold was the first one to finish his dinner, put his plate in the sink and ran back to the couch to finish up those last three math problems. He put the finished paper on the table and helped his sisters put their plates in the sink. Erma washed up the dishes quickly and would check little Harold's homework when they returned.

Erma locked up the house and they walked the few short blocks to the church and sure enough, Rev. Carter's car was in the church parking lot. Little Harold ran ahead to the side entrance of the church which was closest to Rev. Carter's office. Somehow Rev. Carter opened the door just as little Harold was sprinting up the stairs.

"Well, hello little Harold, how are you today?" Rev. Carter asked with a smile.

"Fine and ready to have another baseball lesson!" Little Harold said excitedly.

"That's great! Go into my office and get the baseball and meet me outside in a few minutes. I want to talk to your mom a minute," Rev. Carter said.

Erma and the girls came up the steps and were greeted with a smile from Rev. Carter. "Hello Sis. Erma, how are you and your daughters today?" Rev. Carter asked.

"Fine Rev. Carter, how are you?" Erma replied.

"Great now. I see our baseball player is super ready for another lesson and the girls are looking beautiful today," Rev. Carter said as he continued to look at Erma in spite of speaking about the girls.

"Girls what do you say to Rev. Carter?" Erma urged.

"Thank you," the girls said in unison.

"Sis. Erma can the girls go play a minute? I need to ask you something," Rev. Carter said.

The girls ran to the area where little Harold was already practicing throwing the ball in the air. Rev. Carter and Erma walked down the steps to keep a closer eye on the children behind the church playing.

"What is it Rev. Carter?" Erma asked.

"How are you doing?" Rev. Carter asked again.

"I'm fine."

"No really. How are you holding up?"

"Fine some days and horrible other days but with God's help, I will be fine."

"The reason I asked. I saw the look on your face Sunday and it reminded me of my mom after my dad died. I'm just concerned and wanted to check on you. I hate to ask a sensitive subject, but are you okay financially?"

"Yes, I am fine. My husband and I had insurance. The company also had accidental death insurance which paid us as well. My husband's parents have been extremely helpful and paid our mortgage up for a year so I have a little time to look for a job to pay my monthly bills. We had savings so we will be fine," Erma said. She realized that she and Harold had attended the church regularly but only a short time before he died. In the back of Erma's mind, she was curious why Rev. Carter had taken such an interest in her and her children. Rev. Carter was young, energetic and handsome. Erma was sure that his concern was purely pastoral.

"That's great! Have you had any good leads on a job yet?"

"No, not yet but since you brought up the subject, I was curious about the secretarial position here. Is it still open or have you filled it with one of those sisters from Sunday?" Erma asked as she turned to face Rev. Carter with a slight smile.

"So, you saw that," Rev. Carter said as he looked down into Erma's face because he stood three to four inches taller than Erma.

"Yes, I did," Erma said.

"No, we have not filled that position and most of those ladies are more interested in a position near me than the secretarial position," Rev. Carter and Erma laughed. It was the first time she had really laughed in weeks.

"I could tell that too," Erma smiled and Rev. Carter smiled as well. "I was going to ask you on Sunday, but there was a crowd. Just to let you know I have my two year degree in Administrative Studies from Wiley College. I worked a lot for my father who is the Pastor of my home church in St. Charles. I would like to apply because it is convenient being so close to my house, my children's school and I can walk instead of moving the car," Erma said with a smile.

"Rev. Carter are you ready yet?" little Harold yelled to them both.

"Coming little Harold!" Rev. Carter yelled back and he continued talking to Erma, "Why don't you come by the church tomorrow around 1:00 p.m. and we will talk more about the job, you can fill out the application the board has created and bring by a resume of your own," Rev. Carter said.

"Sounds good. I will do it. Thank you Rev. Carter," Erma said.

"You are welcome. Well, it is time for the baseball lesson," Rev. Carter said with a smile.

Erma sat down on the back steps to watch the girls and the lesson with little Harold and Rev. Carter. Little Harold was having fun, smiling and laughing as the patient Rev. Carter helped him with the fundamentals of catching and throwing a baseball. Erma's heart was full. She wiped her face of quick tears while being thankful to God that she may have a job and be able to take care of her family. Harold always said, 'God will provide.' Erma believed it now more than ever.

The next day, Erma got the children off to school, cleaned up the house and sat down to write out a short resume. She didn't have a typewriter, but hoped she could use the church's typewriter.

Erma arrived at ten minutes until 1:00 p.m. and treated it like any other job interview. Erma wore a black dress and a set of pearl earrings and necklace that Harold's mother had given her as a wedding gift. She wanted to make a great impression. Rev. Carter's car was there at the church and he opened the door prior to Erma getting to the steps. Erma wondered, 'has he been watching for me?' Erma removed the thought from her mind. She remembered how Harold used to wait and walk her across the field to school each day. Harold was one of a kind. She missed him each and every day.

"Good afternoon Sis. Erma," Rev. Carter said with a smile.

"Good afternoon to you too Rev. Carter," Erma said. Rev. Carter stood to the side of the door to allow Erma to enter the building.

"Did you bring a resume?"

"Yes, I did, but I don't have a typewriter so it is just handwritten."

"Well, you can use Sis. Montgomery's old typewriter. I have paper on the desk as well as an application. When you are finished, come into my office." Rev. Carter closed the door behind.

Erma nervously sat down at the desk to type her resume. Erma hadn't typed since college and was the fastest typist in her class. She knew once her hands hit the keys, that it would all come back to her. She was right. She wasn't typing her fastest but it was done professionally and quickly. Unbeknownst to Erma, Rev. Carter was keeping track as to how long it took Erma to type the resume, complete the application and return to his office. It gave him a good idea of how efficient Erma would be with preparing his notes, the bulletin, announcements and any other church correspondence. Rev. Carter also noticed how beautiful she looked but couldn't comment on that given how this was supposed to be a professional interview.

In less than an hour, Erma was done and knocked on his door, "Excuse me, Rev. Carter?"

Rev. Carter opened the door, "Are you finished Sis. Erma?" Erma jumped back startled that Rev. Carter didn't answer but just opened the door.

"Yes, I am," Erma replied.

"Great. Now we can have lunch." Rev. Carter informed.

"Lunch?" Erma asked.

"Yes, lunch. I asked Sis. Spencer to prepare a light lunch for me in the fellowship hall. Care to join me?"

"Well, I am hungry but need to make sure that I am at the school by 3:45 to walk my children home," Erma said.

"You will be. It is just 2:00 p.m." Rev. Carter looked down at his watch.

Erma's thought, 'did he have Sis. Spencer prepare lunch for all of the applicants or just her?' Instead, she said nothing.

"Right this way Sis. Erma," Rev. Carter led the way to the Fellowship Hall.

There was a table already set up with two place settings. "Have a seat Sis. Erma. I'll be right out." Rev. Carter hurried into the kitchen to get the food.

Erma sat down and kept looking for someone to come into the Fellowship Hall and catch them eating together. It was her years of living the appropriate life that made her a little nervous about being alone with Rev. Carter. She was a widow and he was single so she guessed it was alright. In a few short minutes, Rev. Carter appeared with a small cart with chicken salad, rolls, salad with French dressing, sweet iced tea and an apple pie.

"What is this Rev. Carter?" Erma asked.

"Lunch. You are hungry aren't you?"

"Well, yes," Erma replied.

"Well, so am I. I thought it might be nice to share a meal with someone for a change. I used to wait tables in college to make extra money on the weekends. I am out of practice so I hope I don't spill something."

Rev. Carter placed all of the food on the table, said a short prayer and then began passing the bowls to Erma and she filled her plate.

"So tell me about yourself," Rev. Carter said.

"Well, everything is pretty much on my resume and application," Erma said.

"I realize that but tell me something about you that you didn't put on your resume and application," Rev. Carter insisted.

"I'm scared, confused and worried about the future," Erma said quietly.

"What else?" Rev. Carter asked as he filled Erma's glass with ice cubes and tea.

"I am thankful that you have taken an interest in my son. I really appreciate it. I'm also curious about how many other people have applied for the job and when you will fill the position," Erma said.

"First, you are welcome about me helping your son learn how to throw and catch a baseball. Second, this is not the job interview, this is lunch, so you can't asked anything about the job. Third, you want to know why I really asked you to eat lunch with me. You want to know why I am still single. You want to know if I am involved with anyone back in Atlanta or here at the church." Rev. Carter at Erma from across the table.

"Well, you have to admit that I should be a little curious. This seems a little unusual seeing I am here for a job interview. I don't know any other job interviewer that would eat with the applicant and they don't have the job. Correct?" Erma asked.

"Correct. First, I have to work closely with the secretary so I need to get to know the person on a personal and professional level. Secondly, I asked you to eat with me so that I can get to know you on a personal level. Third, I am not dating anyone here in Houston or in Atlanta. When I am involved with a woman, she is it and no one else. I date one woman at a time. If it doesn't work out, I formally break up before I move on. Finally, I haven't talked it over with the board yet, but I really want you to be the new church secretary and no one else," Rev. Carter said.

He didn't want to scare Erma by telling her that he was attracted to her and couldn't care less about the young, single and childless women in the church. He wanted to marry someone with a brain as well as a pretty smile and figure. He wanted to know that the woman was stable, dependable and caring. He didn't mind at all that she had children. He always wanted to be a father one day. Rev. Carter had a great step-father in Pop Thomas as he called him and if he was destined to be a step-father too, he wanted to be just as loving, helpful and supportive.

Erma was speechless, happy and surprised all at the same time. She found only two words, "Thank you."

"You are welcome. Now, since I have let the cat out of the bag of wanting you to be the church secretary, I need for you to do another thing for me.

"What is that?" Erma asked.

"Call me Robert when we are not at church," Rev. Carter said. Erma almost choked on her tea but somehow found the words.

"I don't think I can do that because it wouldn't be proper. There should be a certain professionalism between us because we are still at church," Erma said.

"I understand and yes it would non-professional around other people, but it makes me feel too old to be called Rev. Carter all of the time and especially by you. So, when we are alone, Robert?" Rev. Carter insisted.

"Well, I'll tell you like I tell my children. We'll see, but let's just keep it to Rev. Carter for now," Erma insisted.

"Agreed. Now, can we put all of that aside and eat this wonderful chicken salad?" Rev. Carter asked with a smile.

"Yes," Erma replied and smiled in return. They ate their lunch making small talk about things totally unrelated to church, her plight as a widow or her children. Rev. Carter was taking notes on all she said.

Rev. Carter and Erma cleaned, dried and put away the dishes. They climbed the upstairs to his office to finish the church business.

"Well, Sis. Erma. I will meet with the board on Friday and we will make the announcement at church on Sunday. I will contact you on Saturday with more details."

"Question? Have you interviewed anybody else for this position besides me?"

"No," Rev. Carter replied.

"No! What about all of those people that were at the altar with you Sunday?"

"Totally unqualified and not ready to be my secretary," Rev. Carter said.

"But, you just found out about my qualifications yesterday. Weren't you going to place an ad in the newspaper or denomination newsletter for other applicants?"

"No. I prayed about it and I want you," Rev. Carter said looking directly into her eyes.

Erma blushed and bowed her head. Rev. Carter sensed her embarrassment and continued, "I mean for my secretary that is," he added.

"Yes, exactly," Erma quickly replied. Erma had been married for 8 years and had been widowed less than 60 days but she had the sneaking suspicion that Rev. Carter was attracted to her. Rev. Carter knew that he should do a better job of hiding his feelings, but he couldn't.

The clock sounded with three soft tones from Rev. Carter's office signaling that it was 3:00 p.m.

"Look at the time. I have to get back to the house and then go pick up the kids from school. Is there anything else that you need from me Rev. Carter?" Erma said.

"My name is Robert and no that is all. Remember, I will be in touch with more details on Saturday. Thanks again for coming and sharing lunch with me," Rev. Carter reiterated.

"Yes, sir," Erma said as she turned and walked out the side door of the church and almost ran down the steps to her house. She thought, 'Oh Harold why did you go and why does this man, Rev. Carter act like he likes me?'

Rev. Carter watched Erma until she was out of sight and then made an important phone call.

———————————✣———————————

"Hello," Martin Thomas, Robert Carter's stepfather answered on the first ring.

"Hello, Pop."

"Hello son. What's the matter?" Martin Thomas heard it in Robert's voice. He didn't have to have his DNA to be his son. He loved Robert Carter as much as his own life.

"I'm alright but I need to talk to you."

"What is it son?" Martin Thomas sat up in his recliner and asked worriedly. He was glad that

Ruth had gone shopping and wouldn't be panicked by the look on his face.

"How did you know that you loved my mom?" Robert Carter asked quietly.

Martin Thomas sat back in his chair, relaxed and answered Robert with ease, "As soon as I saw her, I knew. Why?"

"Were you ever hesitant about being with her because she had me and sister?"

"Not for one moment. Why?"

"Weren't you worried about taking on such a responsibility of a wife and kids?"

"No, why?"

"Do you remember me telling you about a young man who was killed in a work accident here at church?"

"Yes."

"I just hired his wife as my secretary."

"Alright. One question, is she qualified to be your secretary?"

"Very. She has a degree and everything."

"That's good, but what worries you?"

"Everything and nothing. I have never been this attracted to anyone before not even Mary in Atlanta. She has three children, just recently widowed and I don't know why but I think about her all of the time."

"Do you just feel sorry for her as her pastor or do you think that you could really care for her?"

"Both. I interviewed her today for the job, but I knew that I wanted to hire her yesterday when she inquired about the job. Especially, when she told me that she had a degree in administrative studies. We had lunch together and it was wonderful. She was shy, only interested in talking about the job at first, but I really like her. She is pretty, smart, caring for her children and has great references although she hasn't worked but a short time after she was married. She needs a job since her husband passed away. It would be perfect because she lives within walking distance of church and her children's school."

"You sound very concerned but I also want you to be sure. I can't really discourage you from pursuing her because I did the same thing with your mother. I was attracted to her on sight and I haven't regretted one moment of loving your mom, you and your sister. It isn't for everyone. Of course, these children's father is also deceased, but on the other hand, there are adjustments that will have to be made. I suggest that you go slow and give her time. Don't rush into anything. I know that you are very passionate when you make up your mind to do something or to be with someone. I thought that

Mary would be my daughter in law but she made other choices."

"Pop don't remind me."

"I won't but you have a heart to protect too. You'll know when and if the time is ever right. If she accepts the position, you'll be close enough to her to know how she feels without smothering her."

"Thanks Pop, it makes sense."

"Aren't there women in Houston that are interested in you, right?"

"A whole slew of them were at the altar Sunday asking me about the secretarial position. Oh my goodness, it was something else. The woman I hired is the mother of a little boy who I have been teaching how to throw and catch a baseball."

"Oh boy, be careful."

"I will Pop. Thanks again."

"You are welcome son, anytime," Martin Thomas said.

"I love you Pop and tell mom I said hello." Robert Carter said.

"I will and I love you too. Goodbye, son and take care." Martin Thomas said.

"Goodbye." Robert Carter hung up the phone and sat back in his chair to say one small prayer, "Thank you God for a great dad."

Martin Thomas laid his head back on his recliner and prayed a similar prayer, "Thank you God for a great son. Protect, lead and guide him."

Erma hurried to gather the children from school and then continue their nightly routine. She felt like she needed to talk to someone and it needed to be a woman.

"Hello," Mr. Jamison answered the phone on the second ring.

"Hello father Jamison, how are you?"

"Fine Erma, is everything alright?"

"We are all fine, I promise. I just need to talk to Mother Jamison for minute," Erma said quietly.

"Sure hold on. Eva! Erma's on the phone," Harold Jamison, Sr. said. In the background, Erma could hear Eva Jamison asking if everything was alright and Harold Jamison, Sr. saying, 'yes it's Erma.'

"Erma, honey, you alright?" Mrs. Jamison asked.

"Yes, mother I'm fine. I just need to talk to someone."

"What's the matter?"

"I think I got a job today!"

"That's great honey," Mrs. Jamison said. Mr. Jamison was in the background asking, 'what's going on?' Erma heard Mrs. Jamison answer, 'she got a job.' Mr. Jamison answered, 'oh, that's great."

"It's at the church."

"Down the street. The little church you attend?"

"Yes ma'am. The only problem is the Pastor kind of acted like he liked me."

"What did he do?"

"I went to the job interview and before asking me the usual interviewing questions, he asked if I would have lunch with him. I was hungry so I did."

"Were you alone with him?"

"Yes, ma'am but we were in the church and I was there for an interview so I thought it would be alright. But, right now I'm feeling a little guilty and just needed to talk to somebody about it."

"I understand. Maybe the Reverend was just being nice that is all and don't make too much of it. I remember that nice Reverend was young and handsome. He may have a girlfriend already somewhere else. You think?"

"That's just it, he said that he didn't have a girlfriend in Houston or Atlanta where he is from. He said that he was a one woman man and didn't date more than one woman at a time. I didn't need to hear all of that."

"He said all of that on a job interview lunch?"

"Yes, ma'am."

"Well, be careful and watch yourself. On the other hand, at least he made himself clear. In my experience, which is very limited, because I married Harold, Sr. so young, men who really mean business, come straight out with it. They don't beat around the bush. They let you know where they stand. Don't worry about things but just keep taking care of yourself and your children and the rest will fall in line. You know we love you and we are here for you always," Mrs. Jamison said.

"I know you love me and I really appreciate it. You and father Jamison have a great night and I look forward to your call tomorrow," Erma said.

"Good night baby," Mrs. Jamison. When Mrs. Jamison hung up the phone, Mr. Jamison asked, "She alright Eva?"

"Yes, she just had a man approach her already. It's a little soon but she is a wonderful young woman," Mrs. Jamison said.

"Yes she is. That could be good having somebody look after her and those grandbabies of ours since we are so far away. It doesn't take away anything from the love she had with my boy. He's gone and I believe he would want her to move on. This soon, I don't know. We shall see," Mr. Jamison said.

"We shall see," Mrs. Jamison added. Mrs. Jamison whispered a prayer and Mr. Jamison went back to his paper.

It was Sunday morning and Erma sat with her children throughout the entire service. The choir sang beautifully, Rev. Carter delivered a wonderful sermon and just before dismissal he said that he had an announcement.

"Church, I have an announcement. On last Sunday, we celebrated the retirement of Mrs. Montgomery who had served this church 40 years. Today, I am pleased to announce that the new secretary of the church will be Mrs. Erma Jamison," Rev. Carter said with a smile. "Let the church say amen."

Some said, 'amen' and others, especially the women, gave Erma an unkind stare. Rev. Carter continued, "Sister Jamison is very qualified with a degree in administrative studies, years of experience assisting her father who is a Pastor in St. Charles, Texas and I believe the Lord has her among us for such a time as this. I realize that her husband just passed away a couple of months ago and she is anxious to provide for her family. We are helpers one of another and this is one way that we can help Sis. Erma and she can definitely help us."

A young woman whispered to a young lady next to her loud enough for Erma to hear, "Girl, he hired her because he felt sorry for her."

"That's what I thought too," the other woman replied.

Erma didn't know what to think but she had accepted the job on Saturday evening when Deacon Wilson called to inform her. Deacon Wilson said that she should start to work on Monday and he would be there along with Rev. Carter so she could complete any forms, receive keys and answer any other questions she would have. Erma realized that there would be good and bad things that would come along with taking this job. She had prayed for a job that would be convenient for her children, near her home and with good hours and pay. This was her job. She was qualified and God had blessed her to be chosen so she would hold her head up and do her best. Erma knew that everyone wouldn't like Rev. Carter's decision to hire her. She had been exposed to church jealously all of her life. It was nothing new and she would survive this just like she had survived everything else.

Julia Royston

Chapter 9

One Year Later

Erma and Rev. Carter had settled into a routine and they worked well together. Erma was timely and efficient. Her work schedule was Monday through Thursday from 9:00 a.m. – 2:00 p.m. to answer calls, type correspondence, edit sermons or take care of any other administrative church matters. It worked perfectly with the kid's school schedules and she could still visit school on Friday if there was a problem or concern. Erma was reassured by Rev. Carter that if one of the children was sick or hurt, he would totally understand and know that her responsibility to her children was always first. Rev. Carter was energetic, aggressive and a visionary when it came to ministry. He was a well-spoken, dynamic speaker so he was asked to speak at all types of events, services and conferences around the city, state and country. It didn't hurt that Rev. Carter was 'pleasing on the eyes' as Sis. Montgomery would say. Because Erma was Rev. Carter's secretary, she also became well known throughout the community and country.

Rev. Carter was compassionate and thoughtful. He wasn't going to rush Erma but he made his feelings known in small ways. Each week there would be a flower of some sort on Erma's desk. No note, no strings, just a fresh flower in water. Some days he would leave a piece of fruit or candy on her desk on top of a small piece of paper that just had a 'C' on it. Erma was appreciative and thankful but cautious. He didn't visit her home but her children had free reign of Rev. Carter's office.

During the holidays, the Jamisons came to visit and Rev. Carter usually went home to Atlanta to visit his family. A few days before Christmas, they exchanged gifts and Rev. Carter brought gifts for Erma's children as well as a beautiful scarf for her that his mother picked out in Atlanta. Little Harold had his own glove and bat and the girls each received beautiful dolls. Rev. Carter had asked several times to take Erma out for a date but she declined each time. She wasn't quite ready for a relationship out in the open with the criticism that came with it. She liked his attention and for her that was enough. She knew that one day that wouldn't be enough for Rev. Robert Carter.

"Sis. Erma, would you come in here please," Rev. Carter said when he opened the door to the reception area. He left the door open and when Erma walked in he said, "Please close the door and have a seat."

"I want you to know that I have respected your wishes by not consistently asking you to go to dinner with me but it has been a year and I want you to know that I love you and your children," said Rev. Carter.

Erma was glad she was sitting down because she thought she would faint.

"I will continue since you are not saying anything. I would love to date you properly but I need to know your feelings first," Rev. Carter was waiting for answer. Instead of answering Rev. Carter, Erma answered the ringing phone instead.

"First Baptist Fellowship of Houston, how can I help you?" Erma said through a very dry mouth and suddenly a cracked voice.

"This is Bishop David Washington, Sr. of Louisiana wanting to speak to Rev. Carter," the man on the other line said.

"Hold on one moment please," Erma put the call on hold. "It's a Bishop Washington of Louisiana on line 1 for you," Erma said.

"Great, I'll take it, but I still want an answer from you," Rev. Carter smiled and picked up the phone immediately. Erma returned to her desk to keep working on the bulletin as well as making other calls. After a few short minutes, Rev. Carter opened the door to his office.

"Sis. Erma, Bishop Washington is here in town! He was one of my mentors from college. He spent two years at Morehouse as a guest professor and he is on his way back to Louisiana. He is stopping by to say hello and will possibly spend the night. What do I do?"

"Well, if he needs a place to stay, I can call the Miller's house and Sis. Miller is always ready with a great meal and warm bed."

"He said that he was bringing someone for me to meet so I don't know. Get Deacon and Sister Miller on the line and notify them. He should be here any minute."

It was less than 30 minutes later and a knock came on the back door. Erma got up to answer the door but Rev. Carter heard the door too, so he was coming out of his office at the same time.

Rev. Carter said, "I've got it Sis. Erma." When Rev. Carter opened the door, a very tall man with broad shoulders standing around six foot five inches came through the door and then a woman with a little boy about the age of Little Harold came in behind him. It was Ida Mae. Erma thought she would faint. Erma thought, 'How in the world did Ida Mae get to Louisiana from St. Charles? When did she marry this preacher and why on earth was she standing in this office?' Erma wanted to run, hide or go through the floor. She had never wanted to see Ida Mae again when she left St. Charles. Ida Mae was nothing but trouble.

'Oh, Lord, help,' Erma thought.

"Rev. Carter! It is so good to see you," Bishop Washington said.

"It is great to see you too Bishop Washington," Rev. Carter exclaimed.

"Let me introduce you to my wife and son," Bishop Washington said. Because Bishop Washington was so big and tall, Ida Mae didn't see Erma right away. Erma stood still and didn't move.

"Oh my goodness, Erma Smith," Ida Mae said before her husband could introduce her and with that wide sneaky smile that Erma remembered and loathed.

"Jamison. Hello Ida Mae," Erma said quietly.

"Honey, do you know this young lady?" Bishop Washington asked as he turned to his wife.

"Yes, honey I do. She is Erma Smith Jamison, Rev. Smith's daughter from our hometown of St. Charles, Texas," Ida Mae said with a huge smile.

Rev. Carter turned toward Erma to see her reaction and she was not smiling. Suddenly, Rev. Carter was confused by Erma's facial expression. He would have to ask Erma about that later.

"Well, it's a small world," was all that Rev. Carter could say. "Let's go into my office and get settled." Erma turned and went back to her desk. Rev. Carter opened his door to let Bishop Washington, Ida Mae and their young son, David, go in before him. Rev. Carter turned to Erma and whispered, "You okay?"

"No, I'm not," Erma said still staring at her desk.

"We'll talk later," Rev. Carter said as he walked into his office and closed the door.

It was almost two o'clock and time for Erma to leave for the day. Erma knocked on the door and waited until Rev. Carter said come in.

"Rev. Carter, I am about to leave for the day. Is there anything else that you need from me?" Erma asked.

"No, Sis. Erma, thanks so much. I will see you on Sunday," Rev. Carter said.

"It was good seeing you again Erma," Ida Mae said with another huge smile.

"Thank you," was all that Erma could say. All Erma could think was, 'Ida Mae married well and was out of St. Charles but somehow back in her space.' Erma walked to the school in a daze. She answered all of the children's questions with one word answers. Little Harold noticed and asked was something wrong and Erma answered that she was fine. Deep down, Erma knew that was a lie. She wasn't fine. She would be holding her breath until Ida Mae Washington was out of town and away from her. Of all of the cities, of all of the churches and all of the Pastors, Ida Mae and her husband would visit Rev. Carter and

First Baptist Fellowship of Houston. Erma admitted that the little boy was cute and probably would have made a great playmate for Little Harold but that wasn't a good idea. Erma also knew that Ida Mae couldn't find out that Rev. Carter had any interest in her.

Back at the church Rev. Carter looked at the small boy and was reminded of Little Harold. He initially thought it would be great for the two boys to play together but Erma's face, he knew he should ask before mentioning it to the Washingtons. They would be staying in town through the weekend and Rev. Carter had asked Bishop Washington to preach on Sunday morning and then they would leave out on Monday.

Rev. Carter led the Washingtons to the Miller's house to get them settled and before he left, Ida Mae asked, "Rev. Carter is it possible for Erma

Jamison and her family to join us on tomorrow evening?" Ida Mae asked.

"I don't know. I'll have to check with her and see if she is available."

"I would love it. We were so close friends back in St. Charles and I haven't talked with her since she married and moved away," Ida Mae added sweetly.

"We shall see," Rev. Carter said cautiously. "Well, I'd best be off. Thank you again Deacon and Sis. Miller and Bishop, I shall see you and your family tomorrow."

"Thanks again Rev. Carter," Bishop Washington said with a hand shake.

"Think nothing of it," Rev. Carter said as he went out the front door.

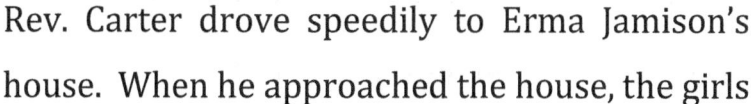

Rev. Carter drove speedily to Erma Jamison's house. When he approached the house, the girls were playing jacks and little Harold was throwing the baseball up in the air and catching it. Little Harold ran in the house when he saw Rev. Carter get out of the car. "Mama, Rev. Carter is here," little Harold yelled while running in the kitchen.

"I heard you the first time you yelled his name, little Harold. I'm coming out to greet him," Erma wiped her wet hands on her apron and put the last dish in the drain to dry.

'What is Rev. Carter doing here?' Erma asked herself.

Erma heard Rev. Carter ask the girls, "What number are you trying to pick up?"

"Our fives," Edith said. The red ball flew in the air and Edith could only pick up 4 jacks but her old sister Harriett could pick up all five.

"Great job Harriett!" Rev. Carter added.

"Hello Rev. Carter, how are you?"

"Fine now. I mean fine how are you doing?"

"Fine. Did the Washingtons get settled?"

"Yes and I need to know why you are not okay with the Washingtons?"

"Do you have time to wait until I get the kids in bed and we talk then?"

"Sure. Anything I can do to help?"

"I do have a few dishes in the sink."

"I can do dishes."

"Great." Erma called for the children to go inside, get their pajamas and prepare for baths. She heard Rev. Carter drop his keys on the end table, the water running and splashing in the kitchen. Next, the broom was going across the floor, the trash bag was being removed and the back door slammed. Erma thought, 'he is handy.'

Erma knew that the only way she was going to get the kids to stay in the bed was for them to be able to say goodnight to Rev. Carter. Rev. Carter was sitting on the couch and looked up when he heard the swishing feet.

"Well, they have told me that they will not stay in the bed while we talk unless they can come and say goodnight to you," Erma said.

"Sounds like a great compromise to me," Rev. Carter said with a smile.

Rev. Carter immediately dropped to both knees and the girls each gave Rev. Carter a quick hug in their footed pajamas and he breathed in the smell of Johnson and Johnson baby powder and lotion. Little Harold had to do something different and wanted a high five hand slap from Rev. Carter as had become their custom. Erma stood there watching the scene with tears threatening to fall. "Come on now," Erma said in an unusual soft voice to somehow mask the emotion. She wanted to get the kids in their beds, wipe her eyes and collect herself before returning to the living room.

Rev. Carter was glad that they all left the room so he could get himself together and return to the couch. In his mind, he needed to stay on his knees and pray to God for courage, strength and the words to make this woman love him as much as he loved her and her kids.

Erma returned to the living room with a slight smile on her face. "So what brings you by Rev. Carter?" Erma sat down in the adjacent chair to the couch where Rev. Carter was sitting.

"Call me Robert since we are alone. I don't bite so would you sit next to me on the couch?" Rev. Carter insisted.

"Alright Robert I will." Erma said as she sat down on the couch.

"There are several reasons. First, I must tell you again that I love you, your kids and want to date you. I want to know how you feel about that. Second, I need to know why you are not okay with Ida Mae Washington? Finally, I am taking the Washingtons to dinner and Mrs. Washington asked if you and your children would join us on Friday evening. I know that is a lot but I thought I would ask anyway," Rev. Carter said. Erma's head was bowed at first and then it raised swiftly with wide eyes at the thought of spending a dinner with Ida Mae Washington, her husband, her child, Rev. Carter and her children. Wouldn't the members of First Fellowship Christian of Houston love that story! The words shouted in Erma's head.

"Well, that is a lot to answer in one night. First, I like you a lot Rev. Carter. I believe that you are a wonderful man but you are handsome, smart and single with no children. Why would you want to take on me and my children?" Erma asked.

"Because I love you and that's what you do when you love someone. You want to be with that person and care for what that person cares about, 'for as long as you both shall live.' Also, I've seen a man do what I want to do. My stepfather or 'Pop' as I call him, married my mother after my father died. My sister and I came along with my mother as a package. He has treated my sister and I like his own children. I love him dearly and can't imagine my life without Pop," Rev. Carter added.

"I am so happy for you and it sounds wonderful but I had a miserable and unhappy life with two real parents. I have seen some horrible things in families with step-parents and don't know if I can do that to my children," Erma explained.

"I would never do anything to hurt you or your children," Rev. Carter said.

"I know that you say that now but I have to be careful. I am the only parent that my children have since their father died. I can't be too careful," Erma said.

"I understand but I'm feeling hurt by your answer. You sure you won't reconsider going out to dinner with me alone sometime?" Rev. Carter asked.

"I just don't think it would be a good idea," Erma said.

"Well, then tell me what's the problem between you and Ida Mae Washington?" Rev. Carter changed the subject.

"I don't like her and I don't trust her," Erma said angrily.

"Why?" Rev. Carter insisted.

Erma told Rev. Carter of all of things that Ida Mae had done back home in St. Charles to prove to Erma that she didn't want anything to do with Ida Mae here in Houston. After hearing all of Erma's story, Rev. Carter replied, "I understand your problem with Ida Mae Washington, but how am I going to explain to her husband why you did not show up with us tomorrow evening? She said in front of her husband just how close friends you two were and that she would love for all of us to go out to dinner," Rev. Carter said.

Erma remembered her father always talked about how important making a good impression was for pastors because this helped them to be considered for positions and possible promotions within the church community. Erma was afraid to date Rev. Carter but she cared for him deeply and wouldn't want anything to happen to his career on her account. Over the past year, she had seen all of the requests for him to speak, lead workshops and a featured speaker during conferences. First Fellowship of Houston shouldn't be the only or last church that Rev. Carter pastored. Erma knew that she would make a great wife for Rev. Carter, but she was too fearful to risk something happening to her kids along the way. Being Rev. Carter's secretary had been enough, being his wife would be a little too much for her small family.

Erma saw the pleading in Robert Carter's eyes. She knew that she had hurt him in private but she couldn't hurt him in public.

"I will come with my children with one stipulation,"

"What is that?"

"I drive my own car and leave right after dinner,"

"Deal. Can we shake on it?" Rev. Carter said as he held out his hand.

"I guess so," Erma said as she looked at the out stretched hand. Slowly Erma extended her hand to Rev. Carter and as he took Erma's hand in his, he held it for an extended period of time while looking in her eyes.

Erma bowed her head first and made only the slightest tug for her hand to be released and Rev. Carter let it go.

"Meet us at Ruby's Place at 7 tomorrow night," Rev. Carter said with a smile as he stood and headed toward the front door.

"I will," Erma stood and locked the door when Rev. Carter exited. Little Harold quickly got up from the cold kitchen floor and his socked feet made no sound as he headed back to his bedroom. Erma turned off all of the lights, checked on the kids one more time and then headed to her own bedroom.

Friday was her off day. She thoroughly cleaned her house. She gathered the mail from the mailman and found three letters. One was from the coach of the little league baseball team saying that little Harold had made the team. Erma smiled and wiped a tear knowing that little Harold would be happy, big Harold was happy in heaven and Rev. Carter would be happy as well. The second letter was from the World Christian Fellowship of Churches headquarters in Nashville, TN offering her a job as the Director of Administrative Services for the organization. Erma remembered sending them a resume and letter of application over a year ago but had heard nothing from them since then and hadn't followed-up because she was working for the church. The third letter was from a real estate company stating that people were interested in buying houses in that area and if she was interested in selling, they could help her. Erma quickly threw that letter in the trash because she wasn't interested in selling the house that she had bought with her beloved Harold. The letter from the little league baseball coach she put in her pocket and the rest of the mail she placed in a drawer where she kept all of her private or important papers.

———✦———

It was 3:15, she walked to school and before walking home, Erma handed the letter from the coach to little Harold. Little Harold opened the letter and said, "What's this first word mama?"

"Congratulations!"

"Is that good?"

"That is great! It means good tidings!"

"Great. I can read that it says that I made the team. Yippee! I can't wait to tell Rev. Carter and Grandpa that I made the team," Little Harold said as he ran ahead to the house.

"Wait on us little Harold," Erma yelled and laughing as the girls took off running after little Harold.

"I can't! I'm just too excited!" Little Harold yelled as Erma hurried her pace and ran a little to catch to up with little Harold.

When Erma caught her breath and they all were in the house, little Harold insisted that they call his grandfather and grandmother and tell them the news.

After the call, Erma calmed the kids down to tell the events of the night, who they were meeting and how they were supposed to act and if they did not, they would be on punishment. Little Harold pretended not to know anything because he had heard it all on the kitchen floor the previous night. The children agreed to be good. They each took an hour nap, changed into their dress clothes and got in the car with Erma to meet the guests and Rev. Carter.

Ruby's Place was an upscale soul food restaurant with tables covered in white linen, chairs with black cushions and the food was served on ceramic plates rather than paper. Little Harold ran up to Rev. Carter as soon as he saw him, "Rev. Carter, I made it. I made the team!"

"That's great little Harold. I'm so proud of you. Give me five," Rev. Carter replied. Little Harold jumped in the air to give Rev. Carter a very hard slap of five with his hand and to show him the congratulatory paper from the coach of the little league baseball team.

Ida Mae could see the genuine excitement and support in Rev. Carter's eyes for Erma's son. She shrugged it off as pastoral concern for kids in the church but it struck a chord down in Ida Mae to be on the lookout for anything unusual.

Little Harold and David, Jr. were immediate friends and played thumb wars and tick tack toe with scrap paper and two pencils that Erma was carrying in her purse. The girls had brought their dolls to play with so all of the children were occupied so the adults could talk. Bishop Washington sat at the head of the table with Rev. Carter to his right and Ida Mae was sitting at Bishop Washington's left side. Erma sat beside Rev. Carter and the two girls sat next to her while little Harold sat on the opposite side of the table of Erma next to David Washington, Jr.

"Sis. Erma, my wife tells me that you two were friends in her home town of St. Charles, Texas," Bishop Washington said.

"Yes sir we were. Ida Mae and I went to school together and Ida Mae attended my home church where my father is the pastor," Erma said looking at Bishop Washington briefly and then looking down at the table cloth quickly.

Ida Mae noticed that Rev. Carter watched Erma's face the entire time she was talking and even when her head was down. Ida Mae thought, 'Rev.

Carter likes her. Erma is about to get another good husband while I'm stuck with this old man and this child to raise.'

"Erma, how long has it been since your husband Harold passed?" Ida Mae asked trying to sound concerned.

"About fifteen months now," Erma answered.

"So sorry to hear about that. How did he die?" Bishop Washington asked.

"Oil rig accident," Erma said. Rev. Carter actually touched her hand under the table to console Erma as she spoke which didn't go unnoticed by Ida Mae.

Suddenly the food arrived and all were busy eating, passing the salt and paper shakers and asking for napkins but Ida Mae still kept a close eye on both of them.

"Erma, we are planning to take David, Jr. to the zoo tomorrow. Is it possible for little Harold to go along with us?" Ida Mae asked.

Little Harold said, "Please mama can I go? We haven't been to the zoo lately."

"Well, I don't know. Little Harold can be a handful but if you think it is alright?" Erma said while looking from Rev. Carter to Ida Mae back to little Harold. She felt trapped and didn't trust Ida Mae with her child but the two boys had gotten along so well at dinner, Erma didn't know how to resist.

"It would be great for David, Jr. to have someone to be with at the zoo," Ida Mae insisted.

"Alright I guess. When are you planning to go in the morning?"

"Around 10:00 a.m. after breakfast."

"Fine, I will have little Harold ready. My house is only a few blocks from the church. I will give you the address and directions,"

"Great," Ida Mae said.

Rev. Carter looked at Erma quickly and mouthed, 'thank you.' Erma just responded by blinking her eyes and nodding her head. From her experience as a preacher's kid, Erma knew that Saturday was prime study time. With Ida Mae and David, Jr. out of the house, it would give Bishop Washington time to study for the Sunday morning message and Sis. Miller would have some much needed quiet for a few hours of the weekend. Erma felt that she was helping Sis. Miller, the church, Bishop Washington and Rev. Carter all at the same time by saying yes. After more small talk, the dinner was concluded and rendered a success. The children were on their best behavior and so were Erma and Ida Mae. Ida Mae had the address and directions to Erma's house and Bishop Washington, Rev. Carter, little Harold and David, Jr. were all smiling. Erma was praying hard to herself that Ida Mae wasn't cooking up some scheme in her mind even as they said goodnight. Only time and tomorrow would tell the truth.

Just like clockwork, at 10:00 a.m. there was a knock on Erma's front door and it was Bishop Washington instead of Ida Mae.

"Good morning Bishop Washington. Is Ida Mae and David, Jr. in the car?"

"No my wife woke up with one of her headaches and so it is going to be me, David, Jr. and little Harold at the zoo today. She is still in bed with a cold compress on her head,"

"I'm sorry to hear that. Little Harold, Bishop Washington and David, Jr. are here," Erma said as she heard little Harold's feet running hard across the floor. Turning to Bishop Washington, Erma asked, "Don't you need time to study your message?"

"Well, when you are as old as I am you don't need much study time. I've preached enough messages in my time to preach a message in my sleep if I have to," Bishop Washington said with a chuckle.

"That is great. Well, have a good time and don't wear yourself out," Erma added.

"They won't get tired but I sure will. I have to go because I promised the boy to take him to the zoo. I love him more than you know," Bishop Washington said proudly.

"I understand," Erma said. "Be good little Harold and do what Bishop Washington says. Have fun!"

"Yes ma'am I will," little Harold said.

Erma watched little Harold go down the steps and into the car with Bishop Washington and

David, Jr. Erma was left with the girls and more cleaning of the house. It was Saturday but she had to prepare for Sunday and the rest of next week. The phone rang and Erma picked it up on the first ring, "Hello."

"Sis. Erma, this is Sis. Blackburn. I am calling to tell you that I forgot to submit our Women's Tea announcement for the Sunday bulletin. Is there any way that you can add an insert today?"

"I could but the bulletin is already done for Sunday," Erma said rolling her eyes to the sky.

"Please Sis. Erma could you do it for me this one time. This is the last Sunday to remind the sisters and we only have 3 weeks until the tea," Sis. Blackburn pleaded.

"Alright, I will do it this once. Give me the details," Erma said as she turned off her iron and got her pen and paper to write down the details. Erma realized that it would only be a half sheet of paper to add to the bulletin so she could make two announcements on one page and then she would make the copies. With the girls in tow, she stopped by Mrs. Lewis' house and she gladly said that she would watch the girls for an hour or two while Erma went back to the church.

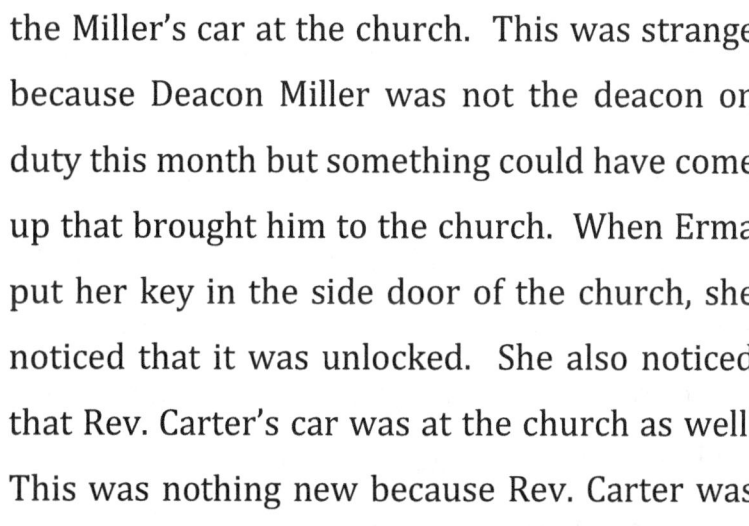

When Erma arrived at the church, she noticed the Miller's car at the church. This was strange because Deacon Miller was not the deacon on duty this month but something could have come up that brought him to the church. When Erma put her key in the side door of the church, she noticed that it was unlocked. She also noticed that Rev. Carter's car was at the church as well. This was nothing new because Rev. Carter was usually at the church on Saturday. As Erma got closer to the office, she heard two loud voices coming from Rev. Carter's office, "Leave me alone!"

The next thing that Erma heard was a woman's voice saying, "You know you don't want me to leave you alone."

Erma didn't knock on Rev. Carter's door she just opened it to find Ida Mae with no dress on, sitting on top of a fully dressed Rev. Carter.

"Ida Mae what are you doing?"

"Erma you should know by now that I always have to sample what you have before you have it," Ida Mae said with a smile as she stood up from her sitting position on Rev. Carter.

"Erma you have to believe me. I was here all by myself, laid down to take a nap on the couch and forgot to lock the door. She came in quietly, took off her dress, unbeknownst to me and pinned me down. She wanted me to make love to her. I told her no several times but she wouldn't listen. I was taught never to hit a lady so I couldn't literally pick her up and get her off of me. Believe me." Rev. Carter pleaded for Erma to understand. What Rev. Carter didn't know is that Ida Mae is as strong as an ox and wrestled most of the boys at school and won. Ida Mae could fight too so there was no way that Rev. Carter would and could overpower Ida Mae.

Erma pitched Ida Mae's dress to her, "Get your dress on Ida Mae. I see that you are still up to your old tricks. How did you get the Miller's car?"

"I took the keys from off the wall in the Miller's kitchen and drove the car over here. I don't change Erma. You know when I want something. I go after it. I wanted David Washington, Sr. and got him too. As much as I would have wanted to test out Rev. Carter, he didn't give in. He really does want you," Ida Mae said as she stepped into her dress.

"Thanks for letting me know that Ida Mae. But, I see that you've got new clothes on, a new man, new child but same old Ida Mae. Goodbye Rev. Carter and hopefully goodbye forever, Ida Mae," Erma said as she left the office for the final time.

"What does that mean Erma? She just told you that I didn't do anything! You have to believe me! I love you and your kids. Erma please! Don't go! Please Erma!" Rev. Carter pleaded and yelled after her.

Erma left the building with Rev. Carter's screaming voice in her ears and head. Erma kept walking numb down the short blocks to Mrs. Lewis' house, saw the girls outside playing and told Mrs. Lewis that she would be back in a few minutes. Erma went into her house and called Sis. Blackburn immediately.

"Sis. Blackburn, this is Sis. Erma. We had a problem at the church and I won't be getting your Women's Tea insert into the bulletin this

Sunday. Have a great life," Erma said as she hung up the phone.

The next call was to the Jamisons explaining everything that happened and Erma's next steps in her life. The Jamison's didn't agree but loved her and the children enough to support her decision no matter what. They asked that she let them know as soon as she knew the full details of her move on Monday.

Even though Erma had told Rev. Carter that she would not date him, the scene with Ida Mae and Rev. Carter was too much for Erma. How could she remain his secretary? How could she keep attending that church? How could she still live in this city? Harold was not buried in Houston, but is in heaven. Erma knew that moving would devastate little Harold but he would have to get over it and understand later.

Erma did not go to church or anywhere else on Sunday. She stayed home to plan and pack. Little Harold had a wonderful time with Bishop Washington at the zoo on Saturday so Erma waited until Sunday at breakfast to tell little Harold and the girls the news. It didn't go well just as Erma expected. Little Harold cried the entire day and climbed that same tree that he climbed the day his father died. Erma felt bad that he didn't get to see David, Jr. again but his mother was the reason for that.

On Monday morning, Erma wrote a letter of resignation to the church, walked it to their mailbox after dropping the kids off to school and returned home to make two phone calls. The first call was to Nashville to accept the job offer. As God would have it, the new position covered all moving expenses, included housing and after school day care services for all employees.

Because she hadn't paid a mortgage in one year, she had a great deal of money saved for down payments for a phone, water, lights and any other housing necessities. The next call was to the realtor who had several buyers to come look at the house that same week and by the end of that same week an offer was made. The Jamison's arrived on Friday to help with any packing before the movers arrived on Saturday. The Jamison's were going to follow Erma out until she arrived at St. Charles and she could spend the night with them and then continue her journey. The President at Erma's new position stated that they had been without a Director of Administrative Services for 6 months and wanted to move her as soon as possible. Erma was to start work on the following Wednesday which gave her only two days to get settled.

In the end, Erma only needed money for gas in the car, food for the kids and a deposit for the phone once they arrived. Little Harold rode in the car with his grandparents from Houston to St. Charles to be loved on and spoiled. Erma didn't stop by her parents' house to explain anything. She had not spoken to them in over a year. The Jamison's were her family now and she was happy to keep it that way.

In the car from St. Charles to Nashville, little Harold finally broke his silence.

"Mama why did we really leave Houston and Rev. Carter?" little Harold asked.

"I told you that I got a new job and it is a great opportunity," Erma said.

"But he said that he loved you and loved us too," little Harold finally confessed.

"When did you hear him say that?" Erma asked.

"When I was supposed to be in bed and I was laying on the floor in the kitchen listening to your conversation," little Harold said quietly.

"First off young man, that's what you get for listening to only part of grown folks conversations. You only got part of the story. Secondly, you disobeyed your mother and that is not good either. Finally, you had a great father and I want to keep it that way," Erma said.

"But he's gone and Rev. Carter was teaching me stuff about baseball and really acted like he liked me," little Harold reasoned.

"He did little Harold, he did like and love you and the girls. It was just time to move. I know that you don't understand everything but do you trust me as your mother?"

"Of course, mama," little Harold said.

"Then that's it. I know you will miss him and maybe you can write him when we get settled but for now we are on an exciting adventure. New things, people and places! We are starting fresh," Erma tried to sound excited, enthusiastic and upbeat. Little Harold wasn't convinced and wouldn't be for a long time.

The Nashville community provided the opportunities, love and support that Erma and her family needed to move forward. They quickly pointed out the best schools, the best churches, found little Harold a little league team and there was an after school program in Erma's building to provide activities and a snack for her children for one hour until Erma got off work. In the summer, there was a full day program for her children with activities, field trips, tutoring and meals until Erma's work day ended. God had provided everything she needed in the move.

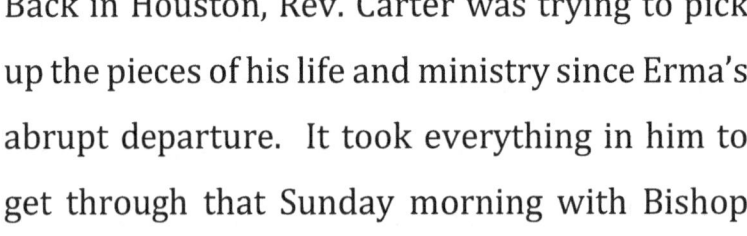

Back in Houston, Rev. Carter was trying to pick up the pieces of his life and ministry since Erma's abrupt departure. It took everything in him to get through that Sunday morning with Bishop and Ida Mae Washington. He didn't care if he ever saw them again. He called his step father to explain everything that happened and they immediately were grateful that nothing more serious happened. Rev. Carter's heart was broken but he knew that he had to let Erma go. She wasn't ready and wouldn't ever be ready with the image of Ida Mae on top of him naked in his office. It was too much for him to relive each day.

Weeks later, Rev. Carter saw the announcement in the National Newsletter of the appointment of Erma Jamison to Director of Administrative Services.

Julia Royston

Chapter 10

Ten Years Later

Erma Jamison was still single and overseeing the operations at the headquarters of the World Fellowship of Christian Churches in Nashville. In addition to her office duties, she now travelled across the country to set-up the national and regional conferences for the organization along with a team. There were many hotels, zoos, amusement parks, museums and sports activities that she would visit along with her children. Mother Jamison usually travelled with Erma when the children were small to supervise during the day while she was at meetings. In the afternoon and the evenings, Erma always made time for sightseeing and activities for the children.

Because of her position, she always kept up with all of the church news from around the country.

Rev. Carter married Mary, his longtime girlfriend from Atlanta who finally divorced her abusive husband and begged Rev. Carter to take her back. He was lonely, still broken hearted from Erma and because he knew Mary, reconciled with her and relocated to pastor a large church in Los Angeles, California. He wasn't happy by any means but committed to what he settled for.

Five years later, Erma saw a notice in the national newsletter that Bishop Washington had died. Not mentioned in the newsletter and acquired through the church grapevine, was that his wife, Ida Mae had somehow gotten the deed to the church, would be selling it and the parsonage and moving to Florida. Erma thought, 'Ida Mae up to her old tricks again.'

Ten years later it was now the 1990's and Erma was now overseeing of an even larger department with representatives nationwide. She had buried her father in law, Mr. Jamison and her mother in law, Mrs. Jamison was now living alone in St. Charles. Her parents were killed in a car accident by a drunk driver. Surprisingly enough, they left everything to Erma and her children. The will in testament read, "To our daughter Erma, who gave her all but we could never give her what she needed in return." Erma's parents couldn't express their love in person but did through the inheritance.

Erma's children were grown, college graduates and married with their own children. Erma was a grandmother but still single. There had been many who had tried to marry Erma over the years but she said no to each of them. Because her children were grown, a stepfather was no longer a concern. What really was holding Erma back from love? Her children wanted love for her desperately and talked about it every holiday. Erma would laugh and say that she was too old. They would insist that she could be happy with someone that would love her as deeply as their father. Instead, she was just happy for her children. Little Harold was now an Engineer back in Texas, Edith was a Lawyer in Atlanta and Harriett was a Doctor in Baltimore.

In 2011, after 33 years with the headquarters, Erma notified the President and the board of her intentions to retire.

Erma moved back to Texas and turned the daily operations to her assistant. Next she began working with and training her two goddaughters, Jillian Forrester in Cincinnati and Vernice Washington in Chicago to conduct a successful national convention. Erma's plan worked perfectly.

Now in 2016. Erma is in Cincinnati, Ohio at the wedding of her goddaughter, Jillian Forrester. She is face to face with the man that she left 38 years earlier, Robert H. Carter.

"Hello Erma," Rev. Carter said.

"Robert is that you?" Erma asked. She would recognize that handsome brown face anywhere. His only signs of aging were the gray at his temples. She was shocked to see him and thankful that she was sitting because she felt dizzy and her palms were sweating.

"You alright?" Rev. Carter asked.

"Yes and no. I am shocked to see you here in Cincinnati. What brings you here?" Erma asked.

"I was in town for a meeting with Bishop Sanders and he invited me to the wedding," Rev. Carter said.

"I saw the notice that your wife passed away. So sorry for you,"

"Thank you. I hate cancer," Rev. Carter said quietly.

"Me too. Well, it was nice seeing you again," Erma said trying to cut off the conversation.

"Erma Jamison if you think I am going to let you off that easily, you've got another thing coming. When do you leave town?"

"Monday."

"Can we meet tomorrow after church?"

"I guess so. I will be at Bishop Sanders' church in the morning. Are you coming to service?"

"I am the speaker," Bishop Carter answered.

"I will see you then," Erma said.

When Rev. Robert Carter walked away, Erma was so shocked she did not turn to watch him walk away, but stared directly into her place setting on the table. Frances Thompson returned to her seat next to Erma along with the Randolphs and the other guests.

"Who was that man you were talking to Erma?" Frances asked interrupting Erma's thoughts.

"Girl that was Rev. Robert Carter. Have I got a story to tell you later in the room," Erma said still stunned and dazed.

"The same Robert Carter that liked you so long ago in Houston?" Frances asked.

"Yes," Erma said.

"What did he say?"

"He said hello and that he is the guest speaker tomorrow at Bishop Sander's church and he wants to meet me after church and talk,"

"You mean you have a date girl after all of these years?" Frances teased.

"Shut up Frances. I guess I do," Erma chuckled as well. Erma scanned the ballroom to see where

Robert Carter was sitting, but he was nowhere to be found. He couldn't have been her imagination. Erma would have to wait until in the morning to see him again.

"Did I just see you talking to Robert Carter?" Ida Mae said interrupting Erma's thoughts.

"Did you?" Erma asked sarcastically.

"Frances did you see it?" Ida Mae asked Frances.

"I didn't see nothing," Frances answered truthfully.

"Oh okay, so ya'll both gonna play dumb," Ida Mae replied.

"I guess we are," Erma said.

"Come on Ruby let's get away from these two," Ida Mae said as they returned to their table.

"Thanks Frances I needed that. As my kids say, 'you had my back on that one.' It wasn't very nice and probably not Christian like but it was the truth," Erma smiled.

"Exactly," Frances agreed with a smile.

The wedding reception was heavenly from the food, to the music, the dancing, the laughter and many tears. Jillian sang to Byron at the reception. Bishop Randolph danced with Jillian for the father/daughter dance because Jillian's father passed away. Byron danced with Jillian's mother and his mother on two separate songs. Everyone was thankful for tissues, the table napkins and make up kits to fix their faces after all of the tears.

The bride and groom greeted each guest before leaving in a beautiful limousine to an airport hotel for the night before leaving for Hawaii the next day for two weeks. Bishop and Mrs. Randolph also bid them all good night because they would rise early to go home the next morning. Vernice and Myron acted as host and hostess until all the guests left the reception.

———◆———

Once at the hotel, Erma and Frances talked for more than an hour about Robert Carter. Erma didn't know how she would sleep, but she did.

Erma had a strange dream that Harold visited her and he told her 'to go for it' because she had been single long enough. He said, 'be happy.' In the dream, Harold was as handsome as the day she married him with his smile and clothes literally gleaming. When the dream ended, Erma's alarm clock went off and it was 8:30 a.m.

———◆———

The wedding flowers in the sanctuary were in full bloom and beautiful! There were guests from the wedding who attended the service. To Erma's dismay, Ida Mae and Ruby were among them. The hospitality was gracious, the choir sang beautifully and then the moment of truth, the introduction of Rev. or now Bishop Carter by Bishop Sanders.

"Thank you Bishop Sanders for that introduction and good Sunday morning to all of you who have gathered in our Father's name to celebrate and worship Him. I indeed count it an honor and privilege to be here today. I am so glad that a very special person to me is in the audience. She is Sis. Erma Jamison. Most of you know her as the conference organizer extraordinaire. But, before she was the nation's best conference administrator, she was my secretary in a small church in Houston, TX. It is a pleasure seeing her today and my question to her and all of you is, Are You Ready Now?" Bishop Carter asked looking directly at Erma when he said it.

To the audience he said, "Turn to your neighbor and ask them, Are You Ready Now?"

Bishop Carter turned his attention away from Erma and began his sermon. Needless to say, Erma heard nothing he said past that initial question. She just kept asking herself that over and over again. From the dream to Bishop Carter asking if she was ready, was almost too much. At the conclusion of his message, the altar was filled with people who were ready. Erma needed to take herself to the altar to pray to get ready. Ready or not, Erma had a feeling that Bishop Carter would be approaching her soon about being ready.

At the end of service, Ida Mae walked over to Erma and waited until several people greeted her. When it was Ida Mae's turn, Erma whispered a prayer to herself, 'Lord, help me.'

"Erma I know that look and I deserve it but listen to me. I have two things to say to you. First, I am so sorry for all of the horrible things that I have ever done or said to deprive you of any happiness. I have been horrible to you when you were a true friend to me. I am old and could die any day but I need you to forgive me. Second, Bishop Carter still loves you after all of these years. Don't deny yourself any happiness based on anything I've done. He did nothing that day but try to get me off of him. I was wrong and again please forgive me," Ida Mae waited along with their friend Ruby Williams for Erma to answer. Frances Thompson saw the whole encounter from across the room and kept a close eye on her friend.

"I forgive you Ida Mae. I'm old as well and heaven has got to be my home," Erma said as she hugged her. Ida Mae and Ruby walked away and Erma did not see them anymore. Bishop Sander's assistant was sent to ask Erma if she would have dinner with Bishop Sander's family after service along with Bishop Carter.

Erma replied, "Thank you so much but I came with Myron Randolph and the Thompsons. I guess I need to check with them before I make a decision."

The assistant replied, "They are invited as well but Bishop Sanders is requesting that you ride in the car with them to the restaurant."

Erma smiled and thought to herself, 'That sounds like Robert Carter's doing.' Erma Jamison had been around church and organization events long enough to smell a set up.

"That's fine, but I'll let them know," Erma said nervously.

"Ma'am, they already know," the assistant replied.

Erma turned toward the back of the church to the waving hands and smiling faces of Vernice, Myron and her longtime friend, Frances Thompson mouthed to her, 'I told you.'

"Well, lead the way sir," Erma grabbed her purse while trying to keep her balance and footing to the office.

Once at the office, she was met by Sis. Sanders who greeted her with a tight hug and in her ear said, "I hope you are ready."

Erma replied, "I keep hearing that over and over again for some reason." Both women laughed immediately. Shortly, the office door opened and out stepped Bishop Robert Carter, Bishop Sanders and the assistant who would drive. Sis. Sanders took Erma by the hand and led her to the car that would take them to the restaurant. Unbeknownst to Erma, there were two large identical SUVs. The driver opened the rear door of one SUV and assisted Erma to get in and sit down. When the door closed, the other door opened but it wasn't Sis. Sanders, it was Bishop Carter. It had been arranged for Erma to ride with Bishop Carter alone. The Sanders were riding in a different car.

The driver played soft smooth jazz on the satellite radio to allow Erma and Robert Carter to talk privately.

"Thank you for agreeing to have dinner with us today," Robert said.

"I don't think I had a choice," Erma said.

"Well, yes you had a choice but no you really didn't have a choice. After I found out that you were in town, I had to see you. After seeing you once, I knew that I had to see you again and want to spend time with you this evening, if that is okay with you?" Robert waited for an answer.

"Yes, that is fine," Erma couldn't believe her mouth said the words but it was true because her ears heard them too.

"When do you leave town again?" Robert asked.

"Tomorrow on a noon flight back to Houston," Erma answered.

"What airline?"

"Delta."

"Where are you staying?"

"At the Marriott downtown. Why so many questions Bishop Carter?"

"First, I am not Bishop Carter right now, call me Robert please. Second, I let you get away from me once, but never again. Are you ready?" Robert asked.

"Ready as I will ever be," Erma replied.

———————◆———————

There was a private dining room set up for them at one of Erma's favorite restaurants, *Montgomery Inn*. The Sanders had a son who was friends with Vernice's son, David, Jr. and they invited more friends and it was quite a large party. The conversation throughout the meal was light, fun and friendly. Robert recalled several occasions of being a young pastor and how Erma helped him greatly as his secretary. Erma just smiled in return but added little to the conversation. Frances winked at Erma several times from the opposite end of the table to encourage her to relax and enjoy herself. Erma smiled back but was out of her comfort zone.

When the meal was ended and they headed toward the door, Erma didn't assume that she was riding back with Bishop Carter so she stood at the bottom of the stairs waiting for instructions. Frances and Vernice watched close by. Sis. Sanders walked over to Erma and gave her a big hug and whispered, "Love you and have a safe trip back home. Relax and enjoy yourself."

"Thank you," was all that Erma could say.

Bishop Carter was shaking hands with Bishop Sanders and two black Escalades pulled up at the front of the restaurant. Robert touched Erma's elbow and whispered, "Come with me."

Erma said nothing, but looked back at Frances and waved. The driver held the door as Robert helped Erma into the back seat himself. Erma didn't know how he did it, but Robert handed her his business card at the same time. When he was seated, he said, "Read it."

Erma read the front and then turned the card over 'Take a nap and call me at this number when you awaken.' Erma put the card in her purse and the driver said, "Where to Sis. Erma?"

"The Marriott Downtown please," She replied.

When the car was stopped, Bishop Carter got out and walked Erma inside. He looked her in the eyes and said, "Please call me. I'll be waiting."

"I will," Erma said as she turned and tried not to run toward the elevators.

Bishop Carter watched her until the elevator doors closed before returning to the car. Once he was seated back in the car, the driver asked, "Sir is she the one?"

"Yes, she's has always been the one," he said as his eyes closed and his head was on the headrest.

A few minutes later, Robert closed the door of his hotel room and made one call. "Do you have it?" he asked.

"Yes, it will be at the check in counter," the voice said.

"Thank you so much. See you next week sometime. I will call prior to returning. Contact the assistant pastors to take care of things for me," Robert Carter answered.

"Yes, sir. We will be fine here. Take care of you," the voice said.

"Goodbye and thank you."

Erma thought she would have a panic attack when she got to her room. She called Frances first. "Frances! I can't breathe girl. I can't breathe!"

"Calm down Erma. It has just been a BIG day for you," Frances said laughing. Erma heard Vernice ask in the background, 'is she okay mama?'

"Yep, Erma is fine but out of practice being pursued by a man. How many years has it been Erma," Frances said as she continued to tease Erma.

"38," Erma said.

"Just like the man in the Bible at the pool," Frances said.

"Bible stories Frances! Really?" Erma exclaimed.

"I'm just teasing girl. So, I have to know. How did it feel being around him one more time?" Frances asked.

"Wonderful, scared, happy, sad, grateful and confused all at the same time. Did I tell you that I had a dream about Harold last night who said for me to 'go for it?' I couldn't believe it. I'm not used to all of this treatment that goes along with being around Bishops and their wives. I almost fell twice because I usually walk fast and ahead of everyone else to make sure everything is right. This time I had to walk slow, smile, laugh and keep nodding until someone else took care of things. I think a half a dozen times I had to grab my purse so I wouldn't open the door for myself. That would have been too embarrassing. Not to mention, that they did the old bait and switch on me. Put me in the back seat of one car and pretended to put Sis. Sanders in the same car only for the door to open and Robert Carter got in instead. There were two identical cars with drivers instead of us all riding together," Erma said.

"The Sanders are smart and trying to protect you and Robert Carter from the gossip until there is something really to gossip about," Frances added.

"Exactly," Erma said.

"So what's next?" Frances asked.

"He handed me his card and said read it. On the back, he wrote take a nap and call him when I wake up. I would know his handwriting anywhere even though I was his secretary so long ago," Erma said.

"You seeing him later tonight?" Frances asked.

"I guess so, 'please call me' was what he said after he walked me into the hotel lobby. I almost ran to the elevators to call you," Erma explained.

"Go for it Erma. Have a great time but first get a nap before you fall asleep on him as he is professing his love for you," Frances teased.

"I don't know about all of that," Erma said.

"From what I saw, you would have to be deaf, dumb, blind, stupid and crazy not to see his attraction and feelings for you," Frances said.

"We'll see. When are you leaving?" Erma asked.

"Not until Wednesday or Thursday. We drove and I don't know when I am going to be able to pry Vernice away from Myron and David, Jr. away from his friends. It's wonderful, I'm spoiled and I love it," Frances said.

Erma and Frances both laughed. "Enjoy yourself as well," Erma said.

"I will. Love you."

"Love you too," Erma replied.

Erma removed her clothes and slid under the covers of the bed falling to sleep immediately. As though she had an internal alarm, she woke up right at 7:00 p.m. Erma took a quick shower, changed clothes, found the card in her purse and dialed the number.

"Hello," Robert answered on the first ring.

"Bishop Carter," Erma said.

"He's not here. But there is a man here who desperately wants to see and talk with you named Robert," Robert teased.

Erma laughed, "Alright then, hello Robert. I never called you Robert even when I worked for you at the church. I'm not used to that."

"You will get used to it. I promise you will," Robert said with a voice as deep as the ocean and as rich as chocolate.

Erma didn't respond just smiled and looked up at the ceiling.

"If you are ready, I am on my way over to pick you up," Robert said.

"I am ready," Erma said.

"I should be there in 15 minutes," Robert said.

"I'll be downstairs waiting," Erma said.

"Great," Robert said and the phone went silent.

Erma got her purse, found her key and headed toward the door to wait in the lobby. She hadn't been on a date in more than 25 years. Even the men who tried to date her over the years didn't get more than 1 or 2 dinners because she would schedule a trip or meeting to attend to avoid them. She realized that they weren't Harold and they definitely weren't Robert. Even though she had said no to Robert so many years ago, she finally admitted to herself that he had her heart anyway.

A black Lexus SUV pulled up at the front door of the hotel and Robert stepped out of the car. He was very casually dressed wearing jeans, a crisp oxford shirt and a blue blazer with gold buttons. Erma stood when she saw him and had to force herself to breath because he looked so handsome.

He walked toward her and said, "You look lovely."

"Thank you. You look quite dashing yourself," Erma replied.

"Thank you ma'am," Robert replied.

Up close, Robert smelled as good as he looked. Unfortunately, Erma wore little perfume over the years because of her children's allergies. She might be visiting a perfume counter soon if this dating thing keeps up.

Robert opened her door and made sure that she was settled in comfortably. Once he was settled, he said, "I want to take you somewhere quiet so we can talk. Is that alright?"

"That's fine," Erma replied while fastening her seatbelt. The smooth jazz was playing in the background and Robert said nothing until they pulled up to an upscale coffee shop in the renovated downtown district of Cincinnati. When they got out, Robert took Erma by the hand and led her across the street to the front door. He switched hands to open the front door of the restaurant and wouldn't let her hand go until he found a table toward the back and they sat down.

Erma always remembered that Robert was a gentleman and generous. They looked over the menu, but settled for coffee.

"So let me start," Erma broke the silence after the server walked away.

"Alright," Robert replied and sat back in his chair to listen.

"I apologize for leaving you, the church and Houston so many years ago. I was scared, hurt, an opportunity came and I took it. Love wasn't a staple in my house until Harold. He was the first person who showed me unconditional love, support, kindness and passion. I thought I would never have that again, so I ran. I have spent the past 38 years serving others. I have served my children, the organization, churches, people, schedules and not myself. Please forgive me," Erma said.

"I forgive you and have never stopped loving you. I was married for 33 years and never experienced the love I needed from a wife. I would have come for you sooner but I have had so much loss in the past five years that I needed a little time to recover. I have buried my wife, my mother, my stepfather and my sister all in the past five years from cancer. Thankfully, I don't have cancer but I am now alone. Like you, I have served the church, the organization, seminaries, my education and all of the moods of my wife but not served myself well. I think that we are more alike than we even realize. I do not want to be alone another day in my life. With every breath in my lungs and every ounce of energy in my body, I want to spend it laughing, loving and living my life to the fullest. I have poured my heart and soul into my church and now they are self-sufficient enough and given me permission to find the love that I need for my heart, mind and body. I want that person that I love and spend the rest of my life with to be you. It has always been you," Robert said.

Erma was speechless. She was in tears and could not answer him but only nod her head.

Robert placed his hand on the table with his palm up inviting her to place her hand in his. Erma placed her hand in his as a sign of surrender and agreement. Robert bowed his head and kissed her hand so sweetly that Erma cried again. Robert held onto her hand and slid into the booth next to her giving her the kiss of a lifetime. Their server headed toward the table to check on them but could clearly see that his services weren't needed.

Robert finally released Erma, found his wallet, placed a $20 bill on the table and he took her hand as they walked out of the restaurant. When they settled back in the car, Robert turned and asked, "How long has it been since you made out with a guy in the car?"

Erma laughed, "In my twenties, about 45 years ago."

"Let's see if it is still as good in your sixties as it was in your twenties," Robert said.

Erma laughed again as Robert came across the console to kiss her repeatedly. When he released her, the windows were foggy and Erma said, "Sir, I am glad that I am in my sixties because those kisses right there would have gotten me pregnant in my twenties."

Robert laughed and said, "With pleasure." He kissed her again and again until it was late and he knew that he must return Erma to her hotel.

When they arrived, Robert walked Erma back inside and kissed her once more at the elevators.

"You are so public Robert. Aren't you worried about your reputation?"

"No, it's the 21st century, I'm very single, love you and could care less," Robert said. He realized that Erma had never said that she loved him. He had waited all of these years to hear it. He would wait a little longer. He knew for sure that she was a good kisser and enjoyed his kisses very much. For now, that would be enough.

"I like that."

"Good. I have your number and will call you soon."

"I look forward to it," Erma said.

"Good night."

"Good night." Erma turned and walked to the elevator. When the doors opened, she stepped in, turned and realized that Robert was still standing there watching her until the doors closed. Erma smiled and waved one last time. Robert smiled and headed to his car.

About 20 minutes later, Erma's phone rang. It was Robert.

"Hello," Erma said.

"Hello. What are you doing lady?"

"Packing what are you doing sir?" Erma giggled.

"Packing too. Put your phone on speaker so you don't have to hold it and talk to me."

"Okay, I hope I don't cut you off," Erma giggled again.

"If you do, call me back and push the opposite button that you pushed to cut me off," Robert teased.

"Hey I'm not that bad. My granddaughter just showed me how to do it a few months ago." Erma was successful, "I did it!" Erma laughed again and realized how much she had laughed in the few hours that she had spent with Robert.

"That is wonderful. Now I think that you are ready for brain surgery," Robert said.

"Funny," Erma said.

"I must ask. How is little Harold?" Robert asked.

"He is wonderful. He is a handsome, successful all grown up Harold, Jr. now. He is an engineer living in Dallas with a beautiful wife and two children."

"His father would have been so proud and I am too. Did he ever play baseball?"

"Yes, that was the first thing that I had to find when I moved to Nashville. He played all the way through high school. He credits you for that. It took him months to get over leaving Houston and you."

"I cried for months myself. I prayed for him every day and started a church team that year to somehow pay tribute to little Harold and my lessons. We had a winning team too and for three years after that. The church came open in California and I moved. Have you been to the church since you moved back to Houston?"

"Not once,"

"I totally understand,"

"That is one of the main reasons why I left. I just couldn't stay in the same city or go to that same little church. I just had to start over,"

"I understand,"

Robert asked about Edith and Harriet as well and they talked about their lives until past midnight.

"I have an idea,"

"What?"

"Since I'm going to the airport in the morning. Why don't we ride together? I don't have much luggage and I have a big car."

"Sounds fine to me. What time?"

"I'll pick you up at 9. I have to turn in the car and we have to get through security."

"Great. I'll be ready," Erma said.

Robert yawned and Erma heard it.

"Okay, you have yawned twice now in the past 20 minutes. I have to let you go,"

"Yes, I have to get some sleep but know that I am never letting you go," Robert said and Erma's insides did a flip flop and he continued, "Of course, I have preached a sermon, eaten some good food, been around great company, enjoyed passionate kisses and I'm in a relaxing bed, alone."

Erma giggled again and said, "Oh my. Help me Jesus."

Robert laughed with a deep sexy tone and said, "He will. Good night and see you in the morning."

"Good night to you as well," Erma said.

When Erma turned off her phone, she turned her face into her pillow and said out loud, "What is going on Jesus and what did I do to deserve this?" There was only silence but she laughed again and fell quickly to sleep.

Robert on the other hand prayed into his pillow, "Lord help me to make that woman fall in love with me as much as I love her." Sleep came just as easy to him.

Chapter 11

The next day, Robert knocked on Room 407 at exactly 9:00 a.m.

Erma opened the door smiling and said, "Good morning."

"Good morning, you look beautiful."

"Thank you. You are quite handsome yourself,"

"Thank you. Ready to go?"

"Yes, I am. I need to get my purse." Erma got her purse and Robert took the bag next to the door. They proceeded to the elevator and everything fit easily in his car.

When Robert opened the car door, he said, "I didn't know what you took in your coffee, so I just brought a little of everything. Cream, sugar, sweetener and me if necessary. Have you eaten breakfast?"

"No," Erma replied with a chuckle.

"Great. I brought you a Danish too if that's alright?"

"Perfect," Erma said as her stomach growled.

"Not a moment too soon by your stomach noise," Robert teased.

"Exactly. Sorry that was loud," Erma laughed.

"No problem. It happens," Robert said.

They rode down the highway in silence with the smooth jazz playing in the background while Erma finished her Danish and drank her coffee.

"Do you like jazz Erma?" Robert asked.

"Love it. I love music period. I can't sing a lick but love to hear it done well. One of the great things about living in Nashville is there is every kind of music being created, recorded and performed."

"Great because as you can tell, I love it too." Robert kept that in his mental database.

He pulled up to the terminal and put their bags on the curb. Erma said that she would wait until he returned. They proceeded to the counter to get boarding passes, check in luggage and head to security. Robert let Erma go first and when she got to the counter the agent said, "Ms. Jamison you have been upgraded to first class,"

"Oh really, how much is that?"

"Nothing, the fee has been taken care of," the agent said.

"Thank you. I appreciate it,"

"You are quite welcome. You will be called in the first group to board the plane and here is your boarding pass. Have a great flight."

"Thank you." Erma said thankful for her frequent flyer points.

Erma left the ticket counter and waited off to the side until Robert checked his bag and got his boarding pass.

"Mr. Carter I see that your ticket has been changed but all is in order. Here is your boarding pass and have a great flight," the agent said.

"Thank you very much," Robert said.

It was Monday, the security line was long, but they had arrived early. When they exited the security area, Erma asked, "What gate are you leaving from?"

"A14,"

"A14? So am I? You are not going back to California?"

"Not right now. I am going to Houston with you,"

"What?"

"Yes, I told you I was never letting you go and meant it. I am going to check into a hotel and spend as much time with you as you will let me. I probably should have told you sooner but didn't want to scare you or allow you time to think about it. I love you and I meant it. My plan is to treat you so well that you will never want me to leave. I promise you that," Robert said.

Erma was shocked. She had no idea that he had changed his travel plans. Like her, he was single and could do that.

"What about your church?"

"They'll be fine. It's my time and I'm going for it. You ready?"

"I am ready I think."

"You think or you know?"

"I know but we'll talk more on the plane. I suspect that you have the seat next to me and that was the reason why I was mysteriously upgraded to first class."

"Guilty as charged," Robert said with a smile and his hand extended to her. She placed her hand in his and their journey began at gate A14.

The service in first class is excellent and just as Erma suspected they were seated in A1 and B1. Erma was trying to enjoy it all, think and talk at the same time.

Once the plane took off, Robert turned to Erma and asked, "After 38 years, why are you still not ready?"

"I guess first, because I have been alone so long. Finally, how do I say this?"

"Just say it."

"Your status of living is so different than mine. You live in LA. I live in Houston. You are a pastor. I have served pastors for years. If our relationship continues as I think it will, my life will change. Fitting in with your friends, churches, other Pastors and their wives would be so different from the way I live. I do not want to embarrass or disappoint you in any way so I'm just concerned. Does that make sense?" Erma said.

'Here it is right here,' Robert thought. She loves me but doesn't think she is good enough to be with me. Was this the real reason why she left him so many years ago?

"Embarrass or disappoint me? Where is that coming from?" Robert pressed.

"I know I told you how I was raised, but after Harold died, I found the most confidence in my work. I worked to raise my children, provide a good life for them and extremely proud of what they have accomplished."

"But," Robert interjected.

"I lack self-confidence. Look at it from my point of view. All of the activities that happened this weekend, I am usually the point person to make those things happen. This weekend, all of those things were done for me."

"So you don't think that you deserve that?"

"Well maybe deserve is not the right word as much as not used to that type of treatment. When we first met you were a Reverend. Now you have a doctorate, a church with several hundred members and a Bishop presiding over 50 churches. I have a great job consulting, an associate degree, 3 gorgeous children and six grandchildren. How does that compare? Are we on the same level Robert?"

"I don't know what level you are talking about. Have you forgotten that you were my secretary and helped put me in position to have a doctorate, be a Bishop and have a church of several hundred members? I may have the titles of Bishop, pastor and Ph.D., but I haven't been truly loved in the past 30 years. My wife never enjoyed my kisses or returned my kisses with the same fervor as you did this weekend. To think that I have had a staff who loved and supported me more than the woman I slept with each night. We had sex on anniversaries and special occasions. I stayed and put up with it because it was the right thing to do. It was proper. It was good judgment. My mom and stepfather wanted me to be happy and would have loved me no matter what but I didn't do it. My wife used my position to spend my money to buy clothes, jewelry and perks of being a Bishop's wife. Material things didn't build a loving relationship, recover her health or keep her from dying. From the start, she lied and told me that she wanted what I wanted. She said that she wanted children but had had a hysterectomy years earlier after complications from an abortion. I didn't find out until we were married five years and suggested that we go to a doctor. I could have divorced her in Houston and went our separate ways, but I needed help. She wasn't you but she was good administratively and organizationally. So in my mind, she became my personal secretary instead of my wife. She became a business partner instead of a lover. She became an editor instead of my best friend. I buried myself in work until I could hardly see to get home. I ate dinners out because she didn't like to cook and then collapsed into bed. I did that for 30 years. I have been training my staff and other leaders to run the church so I could actually be with the person I should have chased 38 years earlier, you! Surprisingly enough, we have both been working so hard that we stopped working on what mattered most, ourselves."

Erma said nothing. Tears were streaming down her face from his words. Robert took the warm towel from his tray table and wiped her tears. Erma couldn't help but respond. She took his face in her hands and kissed him sweetly. Robert returned her kiss gladly. She laid her head on his shoulder and whispered in his ear, "I have always loved you." She finally spoke the words. It was Robert's turn to shed tears.

The pilot came over the intercom, "We are making our final decent into Houston. We should be on the ground in the next 20 minutes."

When Erma drove her car out of the long term parking lot, she asked Robert, "Where are you staying?"

"I really don't know yet," Robert said.

"Let's go to the grocery store and get some food. I'll cook and then we will decide later," Erma said.

"Now, that is a plan. I better check my seatbelt because I don't know about your driving skills," Robert said with a smile.

"Hey now," Erma giggled as she pulled onto the highway.

Erma realized that Robert probably hadn't had a home cooked meal in years. She was actually going to be cooking for her love, Robert Carter.

In the grocery store, Robert nearly broke down pushing the basket while Erma filled it. He would have given anything to grocery shop with her years earlier. Anything to have been in her presence. Erma asked Robert if he was allergic to or didn't like any foods.

He replied, "Not one thing."

Erma smiled and said, "Great."

She could shop with ease. Robert would not let Erma pay for the groceries since she was cooking. Erma let him win that round.

———◦◦◦———

Robert helped her bring the groceries into the house which felt good and odd at the same time.

She cooked a spread for an army. Fried catfish, fried potatoes, cole slaw, hot water cornbread, a fruit salad and a pound cake that was baking in the oven for dessert. The house smelled incredible. He hadn't smelled these smells since living at home with his mother. Robert realized that it was the little things that he missed so much. He tried to help Erma in the kitchen but seemed to be getting in her way more than anything. She didn't mind but it was different. Being around her made him smile and Erma smiled too.

"What else can I do?" Robert asked.

"Nothing else, I'm fine. Do you want to watch TV?"

"No, I'd rather bug you,"

Erma laughed and said, "That is fine. I'm okay with being bugged. So are you a fly or mosquito?"

"Mosquito. I like to taste you,"

"Oh Bishop. You are being bad,"

"Remember Robert please,"

"I remember but you know I'm teasing?"

"Yes, but don't remind me," Robert said with a slight frown.

"Do you need to make a call? That's perfectly fine. I understand."

"I don't have to but I think I should at least tell them I landed safely," Robert thought.

"Go ahead. There's a few minutes on the potatoes so go to the patio or the living room." Robert opened the sliding glass door, sat in a chair and dialed his assistant.

"Hello."

"Sam just checking in to let you know that I arrived safely."

"Great. Good to hear from you. Everything is taken care of for service Wednesday. What about Sunday?"

"I won't be preaching on Sunday. You all work it out. I will let you know my exact plans later this week,"

"You sound relaxed."

"I am and happier than I've been in years." Robert heard the sliding door open and Erma handed him a glass of cold lemonade. He mouthed to her, 'thank you.' He put the glass on a nearby table and kissed her hand. Erma gave him a smile and closed the door behind her.

Erma thought, 'Is this for real? I haven't cooked for a man in more than 30 years. I have already told him I love him. On the other hand, he has told me that he loved me at least ten times and I'm not getting any younger. Lord, help me but this man is even more loving than I remember.'

Erma stirred her fried potatoes one more time and put them on low heat. She set the table with the lemonade, checked her cake and spooned the food into decorative bowls. Just as she sat the last bowl on the table, Robert closed the sliding glass door with his empty glass in his hand.

"The table looks wonderful, the food smells fantastic and you are incredible," Robert said.

"Thank you. Sit down and let's eat," Erma urged.

"Gladly. Your hand please madam," Robert said.

Erma placed her hand in his as Robert said grace. "God we thank you for Erma and what she means in my heart and life. We ask that you bless her, me and this wonderful food in Jesus' name. Amen."

"Amen," Erma said.

They enjoyed a wonderful meal and Robert dried the dishes after Erma washed. After a huge piece of cake, they sat down to watch the nightly news.

After the news, they cuddled even closer and watched a movie. Robert fell asleep. Erma didn't have the heart to wake him, but watched him snore lightly above a whisper. He looked like he hadn't had real sleep in a long time. She found a comforter to cover him and placed a pillow at his head. He had removed his shoes and jacket so she placed a soft kiss on his lips and turned out the lights. Erma left the oven light on in case Robert woke up in the middle of the night. He did. She heard him because she is a light sleeper. It was about 5:00 a.m.

She put on her robe and opened her bedroom door.

"You okay?' Erma asked.

"Yes, I just need to find the bathroom."

"I'm sorry. It's dark." Erma walked a few feet past him to the door of the hallway bathroom. She almost had reached the light but Robert wrapped his arm around her waist and pulled her to him gently for a kiss that said, 'I'm glad I'm here with you.' Her hand remained on the wall but never quite made it to the inside of the bathroom. Instead that same hand was around Robert's neck pulling him down to her while she stood on tip toes.

He released her mouth and with his forehead on hers, Robert's deep voice said, "The dark is perfect." He kissed her again like a man starved. He explored her mouth, lips and tongue trying to remember every nuance. He drew her in closer wanting to make sure that she was real and not a figment of his imagination. Erma's insides went to mush and she nearly fell to the floor. Thankfully the force of their kiss made her land on the wall. She remembered when Harold used to make love to her in the morning before he went to work. The house was quiet and the kids were sleep. It was their time and it made her smile the rest of the day.

Robert thought he would lose his mind. He knew that he had to let go of her soon before he just couldn't stop himself. His body was on fire. He didn't care about church, ministry, California or anybody else in this world but this woman right here.

"I'll be right back," Robert went in the bathroom to catch his breath.

Erma went right to the kitchen. She thought, 'Girl, turn a light on, start a pot of coffee or cook something before you make love to this man you have been reunited with for only 48 hours!' Her body was screaming.

Robert was in the bathroom thinking, 'Boy, come back from the edge of the cliff before you jump.' Robert had lived in the safe place so long that he really didn't want to slow down. He wanted to throw caution to the wind and forget about everything. Instead, Robert opened the door and found Erma in the kitchen preparing coffee.

"I'm sorry," Robert said as he sat on one of the high stools at her counter just to be safe.

"I'm not," Erma interrupted Robert before he said another word. Her back was to him so she continued, "It's great to be wanted. I'm so sorry that I denied myself and you this love for so long. Maybe we had to go through our own lonely hell before we could have this opportunity to love each other with no limits. At 60 plus years old, I am too old to play games. I don't know how much time I have to live. I have deceived myself into believing that I was okay without love, but that is a lie. It is overwhelming to know that you love me out of all of the women in the world. I am so thankful and love you so much that it hurts. I need to be held, caressed, kissed and made love to as much as my body can stand.

What do you say to that?" Erma asked now facing him.

"First, I am going to keep sitting in this chair for right now to calm down. If I come out of this chair right now, it will take an army to stop me from making love to you on this kitchen floor. Second, I want to spend the rest of the week here with you. Next, I want you to go to California with me this weekend. I had planned to go home on Monday but I want to introduce you to my staff and church. I want to marry you. I have always wanted to marry you. I love you. Finally, I want us to get married in California at my church and then take you to Hawaii for a 3 week honeymoon at my house in Maui. I want to love and take care of you. I just want to be loved in return. That is all," Robert said.

"Done," Erma said as she crossed the line this time. She stepped on the outside edge of the high stool raising herself high enough to kiss Robert with no restrictions. When she finished she said, "Get your bag from the car. You are not going to a hotel. I'm never letting you go as well." Robert smiled and agreed but not before one more kiss.

They spent the week enjoying each other all over Houston and Galveston. They went shopping, sightseeing, baseball games and ate hot dogs until their stomachs were full. They went to the space center, the zoo, parks and museums. They listened to jazz in clubs and danced until the owners turned the lights on. They even found a neighborhood carnival to eat popcorn and cotton candy. Robert enjoyed every minute with Erma. She made no demands on his money just his love. The more she showed him love and respect the more he wanted to do for her. From paying for groceries, filling her gas tank, washing her car, helping her repot plants to flipping burgers on the grill. Robert had found love with no holds barred.

———◆———

On Wednesday, Erma called her children to share their news.

"Little Harold, Edith and Harriett. Everybody on the call," Erma said.

"Yes," they said in unison.

"I have some news,"

"What mama?" Little Harold said.

"I'm getting married."

"To who?" Harriet yelled.

"Robert Carter," Erma said sitting on the couch holding Robert's hand.

"Oh my goodness!" Harriet yelled.

"How?" Edith asked.

"When? Where?" Harold, Jr. asked two questions at once.

"Hold on, hold on. I know it is sudden but he's here with me right now," Erma said.

"Hello everybody," Robert said.

"Mama you are shacking up with Rev. Carter?" Harriett asked.

"It's Bishop Carter you nut," Edith said.

"I'm sorry Bishop Carter," Harriet corrected herself. Robert laughed out loud.

"Harriett, mama is grown. Leave mama alone. Mama never had any men in our house when we were growing up. So, if she wants Rev. Carter, I mean Bishop Carter in her house, that is fine with me," Edith said.

"Thank you Edith. I am grown and I'm still your mama," Erma said.

Robert chuckled and said, "That's fine. I'll always be Rev. Carter to you guys and you three will always be the children I never had. I have loved your mom for a long time. She didn't want a stepfather for you kids because she loved you guys that much. I didn't like it but I respected it. My wife died five years ago and I'm now alone with no family. I saw your mom at a wedding this past weekend and didn't want to spend another waking moment without her. I cancelled everything in California and followed her to Houston. I have been here since Monday."

"I have one thing to ask mama, do you love Rev. Carter and want to marry him?" Harriett asked.

"Yes, I love Robert Carter very much and would be honored to marry him," Erma said.

"That's good enough for me," Harriett asked.

"I have a confession mama," Edith said.

"What's that Edith?" Erma asked.

"I found your journal while meddling through your drawers one time. Have you shown it to Rev. Carter yet?" Edith asked.

"Nope, not yet but I will," Erma said.

"I never showed it to Harold or Harriett but I kept it a secret. It's beautiful mama and I know that Rev. Carter will love it too," Edith added.

"We shall see." Erma said as Robert looked at her with a question mark on his face and she mouthed to him, 'I'll show it to you.'

"Edith, do you have any questions?" Erma asked.

"No, mama I'm good if you are good." Edith said.

"I'm great," Erma replied.

"That's what I am talking about!" Edith said excitedly.

"Little Harold you are quiet. Speak your peace," Erma said.

"Mom, you know that I was angry for a long time after we left Houston. I told you that I overheard your conversation when Rev. Carter came to the house and told you he loved you and you said no. I have always loved and admired Rev. Carter and wanted you to marry him after daddy died. I just have one question for Rev. Carter,"

"What is that?" Robert asked.

"Can I call you Pop?" Little Harold asked.

Robert lost his composure, started to cry and in a very hoarse voice said, "Of course, as long as I can call you son."

"Always," Little Harold said.

Robert left the room to recover and Erma continued talking to her children and grandchildren. Everyone was happy and excited for their mother and couldn't wait for the final plans. Erma told them to save their money and be ready when she called to tell them the wedding date.

In the bathroom, Robert looked in the mirror and said, "You did it God. You gave me children and grandchildren anyway."

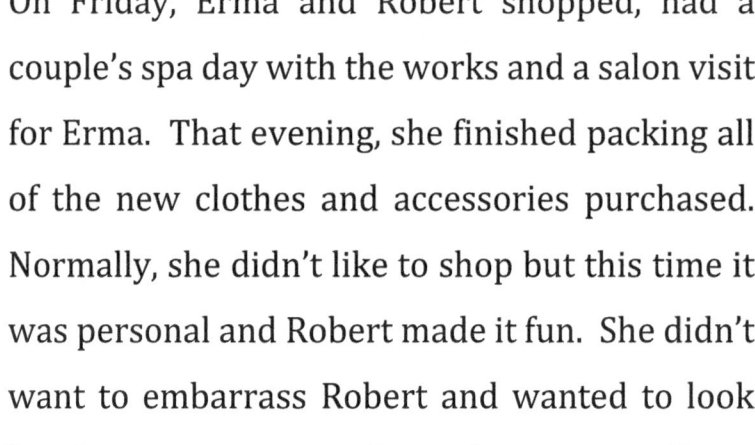

On Friday, Erma and Robert shopped, had a couple's spa day with the works and a salon visit for Erma. That evening, she finished packing all of the new clothes and accessories purchased. Normally, she didn't like to shop but this time it was personal and Robert made it fun. She didn't want to embarrass Robert and wanted to look her best no matter where they went. Erma wanted so desperately to please him.

Robert was so happy about taking Erma back with him to California that he thought his heart would explode. After packing and dinner, they sat on her couch and talked about what she should expect when they arrived the next day in California.

"Any questions. Fire away," Robert said while relaxed with Erma in his arms.

"Okay, I am not stupid and know that there must be a few ladies in your church who have been sweet on you since your wife died," Erma said.

"Probably. So?" Robert asked.

"So, should I be ready for someone to approach me about taking her man?" Erma said with a smile.

Robert chuckled and said, "You should be ready but I haven't dated anyone in the last five years. Like you, there have been group dinners where they have tried to fix me up but I didn't bite. I knew that I wanted you all along. I have kept you in my sights the whole time."

"Oh you have, have you?" Erma asked with a smile.

"Yes, I have. I was approached by several ministers who asked about you and I gave you a raving recommendation as someone to marry, but prayed fervently that you didn't marry them. Each time, you didn't. It was wrong and selfish of me, but I'm glad that I did," Robert said raising his eyebrows to her.

"Me too," Erma said quietly.

"Listen, I am not going to ask the church, board, staff or anyone's permission to marry you. We talked to your children on Wednesday and that was enough permission for me. I have trained my staff and church to be able to survive without me. I must be honest and tell you that it won't be easy sometimes being with me, but know that you have my heart, soul and as soon as we are married, my body anytime, anyplace and any way you like," Robert said reassuring her with a wicked smile.

"That image will be in my dreams tonight," Erma said laughing.

"Good. I have dreamed of you each night since last Saturday. I love you just the way you are. It will be hard for folks to understand but I will explain it when I address the congregation. Be you. The plane tickets will be at the counter when we arrive tomorrow and you will stay in a hotel near my house. This is our last night alone in our own little world at your house and I don't want anything to interrupt it," Robert said.

"Wait one moment," Erma went to her bedroom to retrieve her prize possession and stood in front of him when she returned, "Robert I am about to show you something so personal and private that you are the only person that I have ever wanted to show it to. Open it."

Robert opened the journal while Erma sat and he turned to the first page. He literally walked through his whole life from the day after her husband Harold died, through the year or so that she worked for him, her move to Nashville and every church news clipping, announcement or featured article that included his name. Tears flowed down Robert's face and Erma's face as well.

"Oh my goodness! Why? How? The time, patience, care and love for all of these years. I'm speechless," Robert said hugging her tightly.

When he finally released her, Erma said, "I know, I know. Today, people would think that I am a stalker because I kept this for all of these years but I did it because I love you. I stayed in touch through the journal. I couldn't call you even for conference business. It was too painful even to hear your voice. I always stayed in my room at convention when you were scheduled to preach. I knew what was in my heart. Now, for you to be here with me, wanting to marry me after all of these years, is nothing short of a miracle. Who loves a married man? Me. I regret letting you go even more now than ever. I am so thankful that God never allowed me to fall in love with any of your recommendations. I've been in love twice. I know what real love looks like, feels like and won't settle for less. If I couldn't have you, I just wanted to stay single. I was okay with that, I thought," Erma said.

Robert kissed her mouth to stop her next words, "That's over now. I'm here and not going anywhere."

Erma watched as he went into the kitchen to get matches and light candles all over the family room. He turned off the lights and turned Erma's sound system to the smooth jazz station they both loved.

"May I have this dance?" Robert said as he extended his hand.

Erma said nothing but extended her hand. Robert and Erma danced slow and close all over her family room kissing intermittently until they were sleepy and dizzy. Reluctantly, they said good night to sleep in separate bedrooms knowing that the next day they would embark on their new life together.

Chapter 12

Robert and Erma travelled first class again, holding hands the entire flight. The plane touched down in Los Angeles and they were greeted by two gentlemen who gathered their bags and Robert introduced Erma as his fiancé. The gentlemen shook her hand warmly and welcomed her enthusiastically. They rode in a pearl white Escalade straight to Beverly Hills' famous jewelry store filled with the blue boxes on Rodeo Drive. Erma nearly fainted but held on tight to Robert's hand. It was a scene straight out of the movies. The gentlemen waited outside the car and watched the entire scene. Robert and Erma were greeted by a sales associate who said, "How can I help you?"

"We need to look at wedding rings," Robert said.

"Right this way sir," the sales associate said.

"Take your time and pick whatever you want," Robert said to Erma.

Erma looked through the cases and it was overwhelming. Harold had bought her a simple gold band. She melted the ring down into a necklace that she still wore around her neck.

"Robert, you pick," Erma said to him finally. She didn't have a clue what ring she liked. She wanted to pinch herself for being in LA, in a jewelry store, to pick out wedding rings and about to marry Robert Carter. She couldn't think past that.

"You sure?" Robert asked.

"Positive. I don't have a clue," Erma whispered.

"I tell you what. I'll pick what I like but I won't buy it unless you like it too. How about that?" Robert asked with a smile.

"Great," Erma replied releasing a breath.

"Ma'am, do you know your ring size?" the sales associate said.

"Yes, I wear a 7 I believe."

"Let's double check," the sales associate measured her ring finger. "You are correct. That is the average woman's ring size so we may have what you like and not have to resize it."

Robert picked 5 rings that he liked and she tried on each one. The stones were huge at least 4 carats or more. Erma was concerned about damaging the ring so she didn't want it to sit up too high. She finally agreed to one of the rings that he selected and of course, it fit. No resizing was necessary. Robert selected matching wedding bands that complimented her engagement ring. It was settled. She was officially engaged. Robert took a picture of the ring with Erma's phone and showed her how to send it to her children and they responded ecstatically.

When they left the jewelry store, they headed to the hotel to check in. Robert went in with Erma to make sure that everything was to his specifications. There was a dozen roses, a basket of fruit and a velvet box on the desk. Erma looked around the suite at all of the amenities and was suddenly taken aback by the gifts on the dresser. Robert gave the bellman a tip and closed the door behind them.

"What is this?" Erma asked.

"Open it and see," Robert said.

"Robert what did you do?"

"Open it," Robert urged with a wink and a smile.

The box held a necklace with 38 pearls and earrings to match. The necklace had two rows of pearls with 19 on the top and 19 on the bottom. A pearl for each year they had been a part. The matching earrings were pearl and diamonds to complete the set.

Erma burst into tears again and said, "You shouldn't have."

"Yes, I should have and this is only the beginning," Robert added. Erma went into his arms with a kiss to say thank you and a promise of passion yet to come.

"I got to get out a here. There is you, your kisses and a bed," Robert said.

Erma giggled and was released from his embrace.

"I'll be back by 6:30 to pick you up, alone," Robert said.

"That's fine. It doesn't matter as long as I am with you,"

"There you go again. I am running toward the door but first," Robert took her in his arms again.

Erma laughed again and Robert could still hear her when the door closed.

Robert got in the car and the gentlemen said, "Congratulations sir."

"Thank you, Max and Brandon. I have never been this happy in my life," Robert said looking out the window and called Erma.

Erma removed her shoes and was looking for her phone that was ringing in her purse.

"Hello,"

"Hello, you okay?" Robert asked in his softest deepest voice.

"I'm fine now," Erma.

"Great. Just checking in on you. Anything you need?"

"Yes, you."

"I think I can handle that,"

"So we are talking in code now," Erma giggled.

"Exactly, that's the reason why I am driving myself later," Robert said.

"Again, I don't care as long as I am with you,"

"What I love to hear. I better say goodbye before I make them turn this car around," Robert said.

"Whatever you decide,"

"I love the way that sounds,"

"I'm glad. See you later,"

"Too long for me,"

"Me too,"

"I love you,"

"I love you more,"

"Bye," Robert hung up the phone, shut his eyes and leaned back to take it all in.

The two men in the front seat looked at each other and smiled. They were so happy for their pastor.

Erma waited until her stomach returned to normal, called her children and told them her status. They were still as thrilled today as they had been on Wednesday. She then called her buddy, Frances.

"Girl, Frances are you sitting down?"

"I am now, but do I need to get my heart medicine?"

"Have you taken it today?"

"Yes,"

"Okay I think you are ready. I am getting married!" Erma screamed.

"To Robert Carter?" Frances asked.

"Yes girl!" Erma screamed again.

"Oh my goodness. That is fantastic! I am so happy for you! That is great! When is the wedding? Details, details!"

Erma spent the next hour telling Frances everything that had happened. Frances yelled, cried, screamed and laughed the entire time. Frances asked her to text her a picture of the ring. Erma said that she would try and hoped she would remember how Robert showed her.

"Oh so you just call him Robert now," Frances.

"Yes, he won't let me call him Bishop just Robert," Erma said.

"That's great! I'm quite sure that you will have a few other names to call him while he is making you scream," Frances.

"He's making me scream and we haven't slept together,"

"Soon enough,"

"Right. I have to ask. Will you be in my wedding again?"

"Yes. I was there for you for the first man and I'll be here for you now. Just let me know when," Frances replied and they both cried.

"I will. You know I thought it was over for me. Every day he tells me how much he loves me and wants me in his life. I am overwhelmed by it all," Erma said through a flood of tears.

"I know but God honored your faithfulness. Enjoy it," Frances said as she wiped her eyes.

"I am petrified about tomorrow," Erma said reluctantly.

"Don't be. You are with him. This is his world. From what I saw in Cincinnati, he will fight anyone who tries to do anything to or against you. Remember he told you he loved you years ago, you refused his love. He married someone else because you turned him down. I'm sorry girl but it's your turn to show him how much you love and want to be with him," Frances said.

"You are right," Erma said.

"Walk in the confidence that you have his heart, love and don't worry about nothing else. If he's got a friend, let me know," Frances said.

They both laughed out loud. "I will. Love you." Erma said.

"Love you too. Get a nap and goodbye," Frances said.

"I will. Goodbye," Erma said.

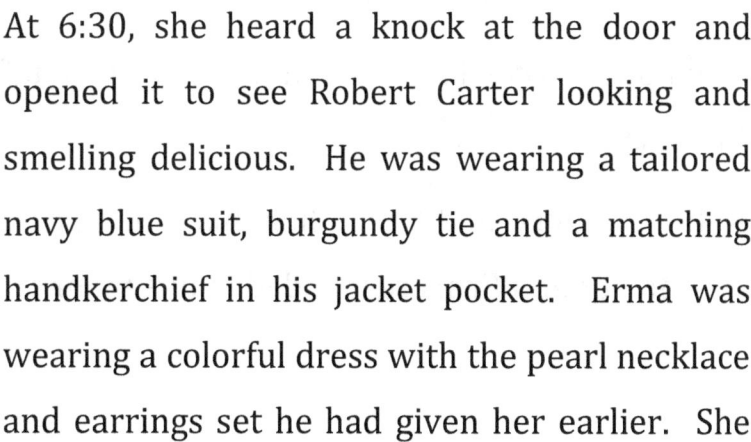

At 6:30, she heard a knock at the door and opened it to see Robert Carter looking and smelling delicious. He was wearing a tailored navy blue suit, burgundy tie and a matching handkerchief in his jacket pocket. Erma was wearing a colorful dress with the pearl necklace and earrings set he had given her earlier. She

had removed the simple gold necklace that was made with Harold's ring and put it in her jewelry travel case. She would wear it again but not tonight.

"Oh my goodness. You look incredible," Robert said.

"So do you. I'm glad you like it. I'm doing my best," Erma replied.

"Better than that. I wish we didn't have people waiting on us, but I can't wait to go with you,"

"Me too,"

"First I must," Robert kissed her softly. "I know how women are about makeup."

"I'm not. You can kiss me as much as you want," Erma said.

Robert laughed and kissed her this time like he missed her and Erma responded in like manner.

"That's what I'm talking about," Robert said breathlessly.

"Yes, sir,"

"Let's go before I cancel,"

They both laughed as they headed hand in hand to the elevator and to his car. Robert was always a gentleman quick to open doors and double check to make sure she was secure before he pulled away from the curb. The music was on, he grasped her hand again and away they went.

Robert drove for 30 minutes to a long drive way that led to a private country club. When Robert stopped the car, the valet took his keys and said, "Have a nice dinner Bishop Carter."

"Thank you Shawn."

When they entered, they were shown to a private dining room with Robert's executive staff and their spouses. There were two other pastors and their wives who were a part of the California organizational leadership. Robert took her to each table and introduced her properly as his fiancé. The staff and their spouses were warm and friendly. When they got to the regional Pastors and their wives, that's when some fireworks began. These women knew Erma from her work at the National Conferences.

"Erma Jamison, oh my goodness, who would have thought it. You and Bishop Carter," the first woman said. Erma was gracious but she knew the woman's reputation for spreading gossip.

"It is so great to see you as well. I solicit your prayers," Erma said as she gave the woman a quick hug.

"Certainly," the woman said.

Erma knew church and organizational politics and why Robert invited these Pastors along with their wives.

The second Pastor's wife said, "Hello Sis. Erma. How are you?"

"I am well. It is great to see you,"

"Great to see you as well," this pastor's wife hugged Erma close and said, "Don't pay attention to anything that woman over there says. I support you, praying for you and Bishop, just be happy."

"Thank you so much," Erma said and the woman released her. Erma quickly turned away to wipe a stray tear.

Robert saw the exchange, came near her and whispered, "You okay?"

"I'm fine," Erma said.

"If you are not, just say the word and we will leave. I mean it," Robert said sternly.

"No sweetie, it's fine. She was being very sweet and nice. It was a good tear. Don't worry," Erma said.

"You called me sweetie, my first pet name. I think we will shut this dinner down early," Robert said.

Erma giggled, "It's left up to you."

When Robert and Erma were seated, dinner was served. Robert said a few words at the end and invited Erma to speak as well. She managed to thank everyone, assure them of her love for Robert and looked forward to getting to know each of them. The night ended with a prayer of blessing over Robert and Erma by both Executive Pastors and then they exited the Country Club.

Robert drove to his house, pulled into the garage, closed the door and four cars pulled in behind them.

"I have brought the executive team here to the house for a short meeting since we had outsiders at the dinner," Robert said.

"No problem just let me know where you want me to wait until you are done," Erma said.

"For this meeting, I want you right by my side," Robert said looking into her eyes. Because they were out of sight, he kissed her and as always, her insides turned to mush.

They entered his house and he pointed out the restroom. He opened the door for his guest and they went immediately to the conference room.

Erma followed him into the great room and he pulled out her chair and Erma sat down. She pushed away from the table just slightly but still was next to Robert. Those in attendance noticed Erma sitting next to Robert so they all sat in chairs next to their spouses.

Robert gave instructions for the Sunday service as enthusiastic, efficient and organized today as he was long ago. She was so proud to be seated by his side. There was a prayer and then everyone left.

"Well, I believe that went well," Robert said.

"Yes, I didn't trip, fall or spill any food so that was good," Erma said with a giggle.

"You were a hit baby and you know it," Robert said as he placed his arms around her.

"My first pet name. I think that deserves a..," Erma landed on the couch and the rest was bliss.

Robert finally asked, "You want to see the house?"

"Are you going to sell it soon?"

"No,"

"Then I will see the house later. I'm fine right here," Erma said with her head on Robert's chest.

Robert thought he had died and gone to heaven on earth. He now knew the difference between a woman with a man and a woman in love with a man.

The house was a huge two story with every amenity imaginable. It was a far cry from Erma's 4 bedroom condo and she could care less. Erma had the heart of the man who owned the house.

"It's late, we have a long day tomorrow so take me back to my hotel," Erma said while Robert placed soft kisses down her neck.

"I could hide you in one of the bedrooms," Robert said softly.

"True, but it's not right," Erma couldn't concentrate.

"I really don't care right now," Robert said as his fingers were making small circles on her arm.

"I do," Erma was all she could say.

"I like those two words together,"

"I do too but I'm serious,"

"I see your point," Robert said reluctantly.

"Thank you," Erma said.

"Listen to you being responsible," Robert teased.

"I love you too much to risk anything now,"

"I love you more, but would like for you to be a bad girl some time,"

"Don't you worry, I know how to be a bad girl,"

"That's what I'm counting on. Let's go." They laughed while putting on their shoes and headed for the garage.

Chapter 13

The next day at 6:30 a.m., Erma stepped out of the shower and wrapped herself in a towel when the phone rang. It was Robert.

"Good morning beautiful," Robert said.

"Good morning love," Erma said.

"You ready,"

"Ready as I will ever be,"

"I'll be there to pick you up around 7:30. We are going from the car to the sanctuary. See you in about an hour,"

"I'll be ready,"

"I love you,"

"I love you more," Erma said as she hung up the phone.

Robert arrived at 7:30 exactly and when Erma opened the door he had a small vase with a single rose fully opened. It was gorgeous.

"Good morning gorgeous,"

"Good morning to you too. The rose is beautiful. Thank you," Erma was smiling and wearing a beautiful knit suit in a mint green color with matching purse and shoes with the pearl necklace, earrings and glimmering engagement ring. Erma's ring caught all of the light in a room as she moved her hand. It was amazing.

"You are welcome," Robert said.

"Did you forget that there was a dozen roses here already?" Erma asked being practical.

"Nope, I just saw it, thought of you and wanted you to have it,"

"Thank you again," Erma said. Robert's kisses were always divine and this time she needed tissue to wipe off the lipstick on his mouth.

"We'd better go before we only make it to the 11:30 a.m. service," Robert said.

"Right," Erma replied as she giggled.

———— ❧ ————

The church was only 20 minutes away which was very convenient. When Robert and Erma entered the sanctuary, the singers were singing and the executive pastors were poised, placed and dressed to preach. The congregation was a bit confused when they saw Bishop Carter accompanied by a woman that most people knew as the convention coordinator. All things would be revealed in time.

The officiant of the service announced, "We are so happy to see Bishop Carter and his guest with us this morning. We hope to hear from him later in the service." The congregation applauded and said 'Amen.'

During offertory, several members greeted them. One woman hugged Erma and whispered, "He is my husband you will die before you marry him."

Erma responded, "God bless you sister."

Another woman hugged Erma and said, "Lord help you, but you don't deserve him."

Erma responded, "God bless you sister." By the time, the first service ended, the negative comments made her smile instead of surprised or scared. Erma was more prepared than she realized. Robert addressed the congregation about his impending marriage to Erma. The congregation applauded loudly, shouted amen and most were smiling except those few. Robert asked Erma to join him at the podium and address the audience. Erma kept her response short, to the point and very similar to the prior evening.

After the first service, Erma was escorted to Robert's office where he directed her to his private bathroom to freshen up. When she returned to the waiting room, he asked her if she was okay.

"I'm fine, but I met some of your admirers during the offering. After the first two or three negative comments, I just laughed at them," Erma said giggling.

"What did they say?" Robert asked.

"I'm not going to tell you because you will be upset," Erma said.

"Come inside." Robert took her hand and he led her inside his office where he closed the door behind them.

"What was said?" Robert urged.

"Looking at your face, I regret even saying anything," Erma said.

"I'm serious tell me. No one threatened you did they?" Robert asked.

"Of course they did. One woman told me I was going to die before I would marry you," Erma said.

"Are you kidding me?" Robert exclaimed.

"Shhh, no I am not kidding, but that is normal. At the next service, it will be worse. You haven't dated any of them, but they have loved you just the same. I can't blame them because I have felt the same way for years," Erma said.

"Yes, but you've been right here for years," Robert said pointing to his heart while leaned against his door caressing her face with one hand and the other was around her waist.

"This comes with the territory when I said yes to loving and marrying you. Don't you think the first lady knows how much she and her children are at risk being married to The President? Of course she does, but you can't help who you love. I sure can't," Erma said lovingly.

"I get it but it doesn't make me less concerned," Robert said with a frown on his brow.

"Did you really think that everyone would be happy for us?" Erma asked.

"No, but I sure am happy for me," Robert said.

"That's all that matters," Erma said caressing his face in return.

"Let me tell you gorgeous lady,"

"What?"

"I fight for what I love. I learned the hard way,"

"I know," Erma said as she gave him the softest kiss and wiped off the lipstick immediately. There was a knock on the door and Erma went in the bathroom to check herself once more. Robert opened the door and his secretary Liz said, "Bishop, we are ready whenever you are."

"Give us 5 minutes and we'll be out," Robert said.

"Yes, sir," Liz said as she turned to allow him to close the door.

Erma came out of the bathroom and Robert extended his hand which she gladly accepted. "You ready?"

"With you, I'm ready," Erma replied.

Robert opened the door and Erma went out first with his hand still in hers, purposely. They entered the sanctuary and Erma tried to release her hand but he griped her hand even tighter. He was going to make a statement. Erma always thought it was sexy to be led through a crowd while holding the hand of your man. One of the ladies on the mother's board yelled out, "Thank you Lord!" at the sight of Robert holding Erma's hand. Robert and his first wife Mary never held hands in public. It was Mary's rule.

After being seated, Robert whispered to Erma, "I'll be right back." When he stood, two other men followed him out of the door.

Robert returned with a young woman, "Erma this is Tracy. Tracy this is Ms. Erma Jamison soon to be Mrs. Erma Carter. Watch her closely."

Robert's look told Erma that, 'This is my decision and you have no choice about it.' Then Robert winked at her to make her smile.

Tracy said, "Nice to meet you ma'am."

"Likewise," Erma replied and sat back to enjoy the remainder of the service. Tracy was not only her body guard for the day, but a detective with the Los Angeles Police Department.

During offertory, more people who greeted, hugged and shook hands with Robert and Erma, but surprisingly no negative comments. Erma was truly thankful.

After service, Robert drove Erma up the coast to a beautiful restaurant overlooking the ocean. He wanted some alone time with Erma away from everything. He held her close, kissed her often and said all that was in his heart without interruption.

Hours later, Robert drove back to his house to change and then to her hotel. Erma was first to break the silence, "I'm missing you already and it's not tomorrow yet."

"I know," Robert said quietly as he kissed her hand.

"It's temporary and soon we'll be together all of the time getting on each other's nerves,"

"Exactly," Robert said knowing that it wasn't true. He had experienced the time of his life with Erma these past few weeks. The laughter, love and tears would continue even after they said 'I do' the first Saturday in September. Erma and

Robert would enjoy each moment until then and the years to come.

Robert stayed only a few minutes and kissed her again for what seemed like the thousandth time and headed back to his house.

As had become his custom, Robert called Erma as soon as he got in his car, "Hello,"

"Hello beautiful, you know I'm just driving along thinking about you,"

"Thinking about you too,"

"Can we meet at your house in a couple of weeks with the kids?"

"Love to. I'll have to call them and see if they can come since their schedules are so hectic. We will see. I hate you didn't have kids. You would have been a wonderful father,"

"I know but you did and soon your kids will be officially our kids," Robert said.

"Our kids. That sounds wonderful," Erma said.

The conversation went from kids to wills to wedding plans. She could hear the garage door go up and go down again.

"I just got in the house. Are you packing?"

"Nope, I got in bed instead. I love listening to your voice in the dark,"

"Baby, you are about to make me get back in my car and turn around,"

"I would love to have you here with me, but you have driven long enough today."

"Thanks for your love and concern," Robert replied.

"Always. Now, get in bed and talk to me for a minute,"

"Yes ma'am. I like it when you boss me around,"

"Oh yeah?"

"Yeah. I can think of some things that I want you to tell me to do to you,"

"Me too and I will all night long the first Saturday in September,"

"Promise?"

"I promise. It's been 30 plus years of loving you from afar. I've got quite a list of things for you to do Robert Carter up close and personal. Right now, your voice is taking me there,"

"Where?"

"You know where. All of the way there," Erma said.

"Oh my. I believe a cold shower is in my future," was all that Robert could say while Erma giggled softly.

The pillow talk lasted until the early morning. Robert knew that Erma would make a good wife and soon a passionate lover, but more importantly she was his confidante and friend.

Robert missed her so much that he prayed for strength to let her get on that plane tomorrow.

At the airport, Robert requested a security pass to the gate. He hugged and kissed her one last time.

"Please call me as soon as you touch down," Robert said.

"I will," Erma said.

"I love you so much,"

"I know and I don't know how it happened but I love you more,"

"No, goodbyes just I'll speak to you in a few hours and see you in two weeks,"

"Yes,"

He finally let her go when the agent said, 'final call for flight 5705 to Houston.' He stood watching her walk down the jet way until she was out of sight. He turned slowly and walked back to the airport parking lot. His first thought was, 'I should have come for Erma sooner.'

Erma sat down in her first class seat, buckled her seatbelt crying tears of joy and regret. She never thought she could love someone as much as she loved Robert. How could she have been so stupid to leave him in Houston and love him from afar because of fear? She could have had baby number four and five with him while building a life and ministry.

When the pilot turned off the seatbelt sign, Erma was the first to use the lavatory and just when she was about to take her seat, the plane jolted quickly. Two overhead bins flew open, a suitcase hit Erma on the head and another on her arm. She passed out on the floor.

Robert's phone rang when he was about 30 minutes from the airport. He knew that it wasn't Erma because it hadn't been enough time. On the line was his secretary, Liz.

"Yes, Liz," Robert said.

"Bishop, have you been listening to the news on satellite radio?"

"Yes, why?"

"Are you still driving?"

"Yes,"

"Pull over to the side of the road please,"

"Why?"

"Because I don't want you to wreck your truck,"

"What is it Liz?" Robert asked nervously as he put his truck in park.

"You haven't heard the news about the emergency airplane landing?"

"No and I just put Erma on the plane and afraid of what you are about to say next,"

"Well, I have someone on the line who wants to talk to you," Liz said.

"Who?" Robert asked.

"They wish for this call to be in strictest confidence,"

"Liz I am not in the mood for games,"

"Bishop as you know, I don't play games,"

"Exactly and I'm sorry for being short, but I'm panicking right at this moment,"

"I understand. Go ahead sir,"

Another voice came on the line, "Bishop I am a member who works for the airlines. I could lose my job, but I know that you just put Ms. Erma Jamison on the plane back to Houston but 20 minutes into the flight, the plane had engine trouble, sudden turbulence and was able to land safely," the airline worker said.

"What are you saying? What happened to Erma? Where is she?" Robert yelled.

"Ms. Jamison has been rushed to the hospital in Phoenix for a head injury. She was about to be seated from visiting the lavatory when the plane jolted, the overhead bins opened and several pieces of luggage crashed on her head and she passed out," the airline worker said.

"I'm turning around and driving to Phoenix,"

"Bishop why don't you wait, get a plane and be there faster than driving five hours?" Liz asked, suggested and provided a solution all at the same time.

"No, because I want my car there to drive her back to my house," Robert said.

"But, Bishop,"

"But Bishop, nothing. I don't care. I love her and I protect what's mine. Call Sam and Sarah and notify them of what I am doing. I am too angry and frightened to speak until I see Erma. Text me the hospital address Liz, thank you for the phone call sir. Goodbye Liz," Bishop hung up the phone to pray for God to keep Erma safe until he got there and for his car to grow wings to fly him to Phoenix. He wiped hot, scared tears so he could see the road. His mind was racing about her children, her physical state and how devastated he would be if anything happened to her. He couldn't think about that now. He just had to get to Erma. The normal driving time from Los Angeles to Phoenix is 5 hours and 19 minutes. It took Bishop Carter, 4 hours flat.

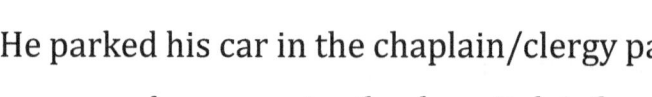

He parked his car in the chaplain/clergy parking space and ran up to the hospital information desk.

"Excuse, me do you have a Erma Carter, I mean Erma Jamison here,"

"Are you her husband?"

"Yes," Robert lied. He would ask God to forgive him later. In his heart and mind, he was Erma's husband.

"Room 205,"

"Thank you,"

Robert Carter waited impatiently for the elevator tapping his foot repeatedly on the tile floor. He should have been tired from the drive but he wasn't, just anxious. He would sleep and eat later. Right now, it was about Erma. Because he was in an unfamiliar hospital, he went straight to the nurse's station to ask.

"Excuse me, Erma Jamison is here,"

"Are you Robert?"

"Yes,"

"She has been calling your name repeatedly. She has suffered a hard hit on the head. She's been going in and out of consciousness. We have her belongings but focused on getting her stabilized and remaining calm. You can imagine the confusion in such a situation," the nurse said.

"Ma'am, I know that you are doing your job and I appreciate it, but right now I can't concentrate on what you are saying until I see her. Can we go there first and then I can focus on what you are telling me?"

"Yes, sir. I'm sorry,"

"No, my apologies,"

The nurse led the way to Erma's room at the end of the hallway. Tears flowed as soon as Robert saw her. Erma was resting peacefully but a large bruise was on her head. Her right wrist was bandaged as well.

"I want to touch her but don't want to hurt her. What happened to her wrist?"

"According to reports, she grabbed her left hand and a piece of luggage landed on it. She has a bruised and sprained wrist. It's not broken just a sprain. She will have to have it wrapped for a few weeks but she will be fine,"

Robert thought, 'her ring. She was trying to protect her ring.' He saw that her engagement ring was safely on her left hand and wasn't stolen. He didn't care. He would have bought her another one. He couldn't replace her.

"Robert," Erma said when her eyes opened and she saw him.

"Hey love," Robert rushed to her bed side and held her left hand kissing it intermittently.

"How did you get here?"

"Car and love,"

"How did you know?"

"Someone called but that doesn't matter. I'm glad that you are okay," Robert said.

"I'll leave you two alone. The doctor should be in later during his evening rounds. Sir, you can stay as long as you like," the nurse said.

"I'm not going anywhere," Robert stayed the night in an extra bed in her room. Robert called Harold, Jr. who conferenced in his sisters and assured them all that their mom was doing well. Erma spoke to them briefly but Robert insisted that she rest. They all agreed for her to stay in Phoenix a couple of days before doing any travelling. Robert called a local pastor with a wife who gladly helped with clothing and toiletry items. Erma was gracious and humbled by everyone's kindness.

"Thank you," Erma said while reclined in the passenger's seat, holding Robert's hand on the way back to Los Angeles.

"For what?"

"Everything,"

"That's what love does,"

"I know but this has all been too much,"

"You getting injured on a plane was too much for me. I'm just glad that you are doing better,"

"Me too," The swelling had gone down and the bruising was quickly fading, but Erma was having slight headaches so more time was needed for full recovery. He couldn't bear to think of her on another plane without him. Robert told Harold, Jr. that he would travel with his mom back to Houston in a week or so. In the meantime, Erma would be staying at his house.

———◆———

A week later Robert and Erma were on a plane and arrived safely in Houston. Robert stayed the entire week and was there when Erma's children arrived to check on their mom. Little Harold and

Robert hugged for the longest time and everyone cried. It was so wonderful. Little Harold now had a dad.

After all that happened, Robert wanted to move the wedding up from Labor Day weekend but Erma insisted that they keep their plans the same. It wasn't about a wedding but she wanted her family and friends to be there. It was agreed that the children, their spouses and grandchildren would come to Los Angeles in 3 weeks and stay at Robert's house right before the wedding. He wanted every room in the house filled with family, friends and love.

They had only 3 weeks to pull it off and they did. Frances flew out from Chicago to help Erma pick out her dress, select the dresses for her and Jean Sanders as well as look at the ring up close, laugh, cry and have fun for a few days with her long-time friend.

"I am just so happy for you. Okay, is this Bishop Morris single?" Frances asked.

"Yes, girl he is and looking for a wife,"

"Don't play with me," Frances warned.

"I am serious. Just think, you could leave cold Chicago and be closer to me," Erma said.

"Wouldn't that be something? The girls from St. Charles are on the move!" Frances shouted.

"Yes!" They both screamed with laughter.

Chapter 14

The week of the wedding finally arrived. There were licenses, last minute fittings, flowers and finalizing everything before her family arrived. Erma was recovering nicely from her injuries and they were seated on the couch enjoying the calm before the storm in Erma's words.

"So you ready to be Mrs. Robert Carter?"

"Nope, I'm just ready to be married to Robert, my love,"

"That's all that matters," Robert said.

Robert rented a small bus to collect all of his new family. He was overwhelmed and enjoyed every minute of it. His house staff out did themselves with making preparations for the visitors. It was truly a labor of love because they saw how happy it made their employer. Everyone got settled into their rooms, the kids put on bathing suits and swam, the women were with Erma catching up and Harold, Jr. and Robert found the only quiet place in the house to talk, his office.

"Well, Pop, how are you?"

"I am fine son and happier than I have ever been in my life,"

"Great. I have to ask you, where is the honeymoon?"

"Maui,"

"Awesome,"

"I can't wait to get your mom there all to myself,"

"She is excited as well. She loves you so much,"

"I love her too,"

"That's what counts to me and my sisters,"

Food was served to the adults in the main dining room and the grandchildren were fed in a smaller dining room just off from the kitchen.

When dinner was over, the adults were in the family room watching movies and the grandchildren were in the play room playing video games.

Robert walked from room to room checking on everyone. To see his house completely filled with family was a bit much for Robert. He walked by Erma and she saw the brimming tears in his eyes. She followed him to his office and locked the door behind them. His arm was outstretched on the couch as an invitation which Erma gladly accepted. With her head on his chest and her body fit snug under his arm she asked, "You okay?"

"Yes and no,"

"What's the matter?"

"God gave me the desire of my heart. You and the kids,"

"Yes, He did and I am so happy that you are so happy," Erma kissed away Robert's tears and as always, ignited his heart.

It was finally their wedding day. How Robert and Erma lived 38 years without being in each other's lives they didn't know? They could hardly go an hour without speaking or being in each other's presence.

"Hello," Erma said.

"Hey love. You know that you will be officially Mrs. Erma Carter in 2 hours,"

"Yes and can't wait,"

"Me either,"

"What are you wearing?"

"A Tux right now but in about six hours, you!"

"Alright now, I just had a hot flash on that one,"

"That's what I was counting on,"

At exactly 1:00 p.m., Bishop Robert H. Carter walked in the side door behind the officiant, Bishop John Harrison along with his best man, Bishop James Sanders and the other groomsman, Bishop Joshua Morris. Robert was wearing a champagne colored tuxedo that complemented his golden brown skin perfectly and the best man and other groomsman were in earth toned tuxedos.

There were two bridesmaids, Jean Sanders and Frances Thompson with earth toned dresses to match the groomsmen's tuxedos. It was a small, elegant affair with no flower girl or ring bearer necessary because Bishop Sanders had the rings and there were flowers everywhere. At approximately 1:15 p.m., Bishop Harrison asked for the entire congregation to stand for the entrance of the bride. The 2,000 seat auditorium was completely filled. Little Harold, escorted his mother, Erma slowly down the aisle to his Pop,

Bishop Carter. Erma wore a long champagne colored gown of lace and rhinestones with a rhinestone head piece to match Robert Carter's tuxedo. Robert strived to maintain his composure despite his heart pounding fast, sweaty palms and a gleaming smile on his face. He had performed hundreds of weddings, but this was different. It was his wedding and he was marrying the love of his life, Erma Smith Jamison.

The music was heavenly and the decorations were classic.

When Harold, Jr. and Erma arrived at the altar, her children surprised them both by having words.

"Pop we love you and mom and look forward to many years of making your house noisy, messy and happy," Harold, Jr. said.

"Pop, you love our mother the way she should be loved and for that we will be eternally grateful," Harriett said.

"Pop, we have loved you since we lost our biological father 30 plus years ago. There are some children who have never known or been loved by one father in a lifetime. The Jamison children have been doubly blessed to be loved by two fathers and that love will carry us into eternity. We love you," Edith said.

Each of Erma's children along with their spouses and their children hugged them both. The grandchildren placed a commemorative token in Robert's pocket. Harold, Jr. placed a gold bracelet on Robert's arm that had each family member's first name inscribed on each pendant. Harriett placed a matching bracelet on Erma's arm and Edith placed a one pendant gold necklace around her neck inscribed with the date and their initials. There wasn't a dry eye in the sanctuary. After the children were seated, Robert and Erma regained their composure and Bishop Harrison began the ceremony.

After the final prayer of blessing, Robert kissed Erma until the entire sanctuary swooned. Erma fanned herself which made everyone laugh and applaud.

"I now present to you for the first time, Bishop and Mrs. Robert Harris Carter," Bishop Harrison said. A thunderous applause and whistles were heard by all. Robert placed Erma's arm under his and they headed out of the sanctuary to the reception, a 3 week honeymoon in Maui and the rest of their lives.

Conclusion

Two months later, Robert and Erma flew into Chicago's O'Hare airport to attend the wedding of Myron Randolph and Vernice Washington. Erma entered the dressing room to greet Vernice right before the ceremony. Erma was still glowing from the Hawaii and California sun.

"There are my girls. Hey babies," Erma said as she saw her goddaughters, Vernice Washington and Jillian Randolph. Vernice was about to marry Jillian's husband's twin brother, Myron Randolph.

Vernice said, "Sis. Erma, you look amazing!"

"Oh my goodness, look at you Sis. Erma," Jillian said.

"Thank you babies. You both look wonderful to me. This is what love looks like after three weeks in Maui. White beaches, blue water, making love every day. It was awesome," Erma said while smiling, laughing and hugging them tightly. Remembering those three weeks gave Erma goosebumps even now.

"Yes, that's what I'm talking about! Happy for you," Jillian yelled.

"Sis. Erma you told us earlier this year that you didn't see a man in your future, but you ended up getting married after Jillian and before me."

"Baby, God works in mysterious ways. I love it," Erma said laughing.

"Me too," Vernice said.

"Me too," Jillian said happily married to the love of her life, Byron.

"Be blessed girls and try to be half as happy as I am," Erma said.

"I will and hopefully, my mama will be as happy as you by Christmas. The Bishops don't seem to waste any time. Bishop Joshua Morris has called my mama every day since your wedding," Vernice said.

"Is he here?"

"Is he here? He got here on Monday and won't leave until next Monday!" Vernice exclaimed.

"Lord, help. Love is in the air!" Erma shouted.

The wedding coordinator came in and said, "5 minutes ladies, 5 minutes,"

"Say a prayer Sis. Erma," Vernice asked.

"Lord, bless these girls to love their husbands, do your will and be all that you called them to be. In Jesus' name, Amen," Erma said.

"Amen," Vernice and Jillian said in unison.

Erma went into the sanctuary to sit next to her best friend Frances and hold her hand as she watched Frances' baby, Vernice get married. Robert Carter was the officiant and Joshua Morris said the closing prayer. When Erma sat down, she looked up at Robert who winked at her. Erma in turn, smiled, blew him a kiss and prayed that they would always be on their honeymoon.

Jillian, Vernice and Erma were the Women of the Fellowship that all found the love that they thought would never come. They waited for the right one. Because when God sends him, he will be the right one, with the right love so you will live the right life. Happily ever after.

About the Author

Julia Royston is an author, publisher, speaker, teacher and songwriter residing in Southern Indiana with her husband, Brian K. Royston. To her credit, Julia has written original music for 5 Music CDs, 2 DVDs, authored 20 Books, a contributing author in 3 books. Julia and her husband spend their spare time overseeing the operations of 3 companies and a non-profit organization. BK Royston Publishing, LLC and Royal Media Publishing to provide quality, informative, inspirational and entertaining materials in the global market place in all media formats. Julia Royston Enterprises is a writing and business consulting firm to assist aspiring authors and business owners get their message to the masses. For the Kingdom Ministries is a non-profit organization that is established to encourage, enlighten and empower people to live the abundant life and walk in purpose and destiny. By profession, Julia is a certified, technology teacher with the local public school system.

For more information visit www.bkroystonpublishing.com, www.royalmediaandpublishing.com, www.juliaroystonenterprises.com or www.juliaroyston.net.

Keep up with Julia on Social Media by following or liking her pages on Facebook, Twitter, LinkedIn, Instagram, Periscope and YouTube Channel.